She is here

She is here. She comes. She is running along the passage outside my room, 'Help me, help me, Matilda. He wasn't waiting...I'm all alone...Help me Matilda.' Her green eyes stream scarlet tears down her white cheeks. The ruby necklet, the shimmering dress. She runs outside, amongst the pear trees, through the moonlight, on blistered feet. She is scrabbling her bitten fingers at the windows...

Again and again, night after night, Frances shakes me awake as I scream out. For I cannot forget her.

Whenever I close my eyes, she is there.

Sometimes I unlock the secret compartment of my travelling case and look back through the pages of my journal. There I am. A silly young child sitting in a pear tree.

Matilda's SECRET

SANDRA GOLDBACHER

A Girl for all Time
BOOK

First published in Great Britain in 2011
by Daughters of History Ltd. Reg. No. 7057626
Albany House, 4th Floor
324 Regent Street
London W1B 3HH
United Kingdom
www.daughtersofhistory.co.uk

I Begin

The Start of My Most Sacred, Secret and Precious Diary, Norfolk 1540

I am writing this sitting in my pear tree. No one can find me here. I can hide here for a full half hour, away from sewing and laundering and grinding up hare's brain for my brother Robert's stinking foot. The page is already a little stained with juice from my pear and the ink has run like tears. But I never cry.

I hate Robert. I hate my tiny little life. Sometimes, I feel so bored I want to climb to the top of the tree and let out a scream, so loud it would scatter all the wood-pigeons in the orchard to the farthest ends of father's estate. A scream to make the dead rise from their graves in their winding sheets and send all the dogs whining for cover, but of course I don't. I keep the scream inside, walk away in a ladylike manner and then run secretly to my tree. Though its branches are winter-bare and my fingers numb with cold, and the pear a bottled one, I can still feel my summer feeling here.

So, I have decided, I am going to write everything down in you, my precious new journal. My thoughts. The story of my little life. Not that anything much will ever, EVER happen to me.

If I write everything down, it will be like letting blood. I feel freer already. Free like I feel when I'm climbing my pear tree. Free like I feel riding my horse, Caspian, along the shore at Holkham, galloping till my jaw aches and the wind sears my skin.

My name is Matilda Marchmont and I am trapped in the wrong life. I shall be thirteen years old, the day after tomorrow, and I vow that I shall, one day, escape my infuriating, beloved family, my mouldy old home in the endless Fens and find adventure. And not have to eat pears, pears, pears every day…

Someone is coming…

This Same Night

Frances nearly found me. I love my sister, but I would also quite like to kill her. She's bossy and nosy. I am writing in bed, under the coverlet, though I should not be wasting the candle, but the moonlight is too pale. Frances is snoring by my side and Kate is snuffling away like a piglet in her little bed, dreaming of syllabub pudding.

I slipped out of my tree before Frances found me and hid you, dear journal, under my kirtle and pretended to be picking lavender for her pomander.

Frances made me go and crush up more hare's brain for Kate's coming-in teeth and then mix the hog's lard for Robert's foot.

No such fuss would be made if it was one of us girls who hurt a foot, and not a precious boy, 'the future of the Marchmont family.' Yawn. How many times have I heard that!? And he was only clowning around on a hunt. He's so lucky to be a boy. He gets to study and learn fighting and hunt. And one day he may even be got a place at Court.

What do Frances and I do but help the servants bake and launder and mix medicines and de-brain hares and do sewing? We don't even have dancing or music lessons to help us find husbands.

I know I should be grateful father taught me to read and write, and that I can steal Robert's books. Well, he's so stupid, he doesn't want them. Many girls my age, from noble families, can barely sign their names or turn a sentence.

Thank God I'm not like Emilia Coxon, poor dreary thing. She's only fourteen and is already married off with two children…Yes Matilda, try and be a bit less complainy from now on.

I need to use the pot. I drank too much small beer at dinner. Piss quietly…Must not wake Frances.

Anyway, I mixed a sleeping draught for father and a headache powder for mother, who is sick with the coming baby in her. She puked over the counterpane this morning and Lettyce had to launder it again.

Lettyce is my dearest friend. Well my only friend, that isn't a sister or an animal. I have Caspian and my puppy Hunter. Lettyce is our servant. She's already thirteen, and is really clever and funny. She came to us from London. She goes back at least twice a year to see her mother and nine brothers and sisters.

She sees such things in the city! She's been to the playhouse and seen the Royal barge on the Thames, lit up with dancing ladies eating peacocks made of marchpane. Her older brother Percy, who is fifteen, works in the gardens at the Tower of London. The Bloody Tower. Shiver. She says he's really clever and is always designing mazes on bits of paper. I think he might be quite handsome, maybe with a lock of dark hair that falls over smiling eyes.

I quite like to think about Percy sometimes. I bet his stockings don't stink like my brother's. Lettyce is lucky. She might not have anything in the world, but she has more freedom than I do.

When I'm making elixirs I feel like an alchemist. I'd love to be a physician. Imagine if girls could be doctors! Even Father says I have a natural talent for it. Sometimes I think I might be a witch.

Lettyce says my second cousin, Anne Boleyn, King Henry's second wife, was a witch and had warts on her body, shaped like moons, which are a sign of the Devil. And she had a sixth finger that she had special elaborate sleeves to hide. Maybe I have witch's power too.

Anne had a dreadful grisly death, but at least she had an exciting life. She could write songs and speak lots of languages and lived at the French court. She met the cleverest people in Europe and wore crimson velvet and a black satin cape in her bedroom. She might have had her head cut off, but at least she bewitched the King of England.

What could people say about me if I died tomorrow? 'Matilda Marchmont. Did sewing, rode a horse, laundered things and ate a lot of pears.'

Frances and mother would be horrified if they knew half the things that run through my head. Especially about court. Robert would scoff and push me in the lake again. I hate him. Sometimes I imagine myself filling my pomander with poison. At the Italian court they fill up rings with poison to tip into their enemies' wine - they call it eternity powder. I know how to make it...so one day, if Robert is particularly vile...

Longing

I fell asleep and singed my hair. I have had to cut some off but, thank goodness, I didn't burn the bed-sheet. I am in the tree. Frances seems content to sew samplers and clean Robert's greasy doublets and plan pear puddings and dream of her own husband and a household full of babies. She doesn't long for...Oh I don't know...something else...

It is not fair to be a girl in this world. I know I should be grateful. I am a 'Nobleman's daughter and distantly related to the Great Duke of Norfolk of the famous Howard dynasty.' Blah blah blah...Terrifying man. I have to call him Uncle. They say he helped to send my cousin Anne, his own niece, to the block.

Mother forbids me to talk of it and calls me morbid. But what must it be like to kneel down, with your eyes blindfolded and feel your head being swiped from your neck, with hundreds of people watching? And to know it is your own husband who has ordered it? It gives me thrilling shivers.

Oh Lord, how the buds on my chest hurt when I sit up. They are starting to grow and my bodice presses sorely. I am sure one is bigger than the other. Is that a sign of a witch?

My Cousin Katherine

Mother has just told me a wondrous thing. My cousin, Katherine Howard – she's two years older than me and very sophisticated and beautiful. Well, she has acquired a position at court as Lady-in-Waiting to the new Queen: the German from Cleves. Katherine's already had an exciting life. When she was seven she went to live at her grandmother's in London with lots of other young people.

All the girls slept in great dormitories and had secret midnight feasts with wine and sweetmeats, and boys climbed up the ivy for parties. Lettyce told me of it – her sister Alice worked there. Frances overheard us and said it was shocking and immoral. She is such a mouse.

We might be noble, but we are so poor we can barely maintain the estate and often live on eggs and pears and dumplings for days, with no meat. Except for Robert. All the money goes on Robert's education and not on Frances' dowry and father does not sleep at night for it. If only I could get to court and become an explorer or a court physician. Frances says cousin Katherine must know how to dance, sing and coil up her hair to enchant men. I just want to be FREE.

Robert, Frances and mother keep telling me I am too plain and strange looking for boys to notice me anyway, thank goodness. My eyes are like grey pebbles or the dirty waves at Holkham. Skin moonish and luminous, figure like a boy's, feet too large, legs too long and muscled from galloping on Caspian, hair too drab. Not a "glorious red" like Frances'.

An Obedient Quick Girl

My fingers are trembling so much I can scarcely hold the quill. My heart is thunder.

I am to go to court! I woke to hear hooves beneath my window and hammering on the door. I crept down in my nightshift to listen at father's door. It was my Uncle, the Duke of Norfolk himself…

I heard him say he's placed my cousin Katherine at court for a 'great reason'. King Henry is tiring of the German, Queen Anne, even though he only married her a few months ago. My Uncle's plan is that the King's fancy might turn to my cousin Katherine. That's why he's sent Katherine to court at his expense. Then the Howards would have a queen in the family!

He wants an 'obedient quick girl' to watch over Katherine and encourage her to advance herself with the King, to give him reports of their progress and 'stop her head being turned by admirers.'

They must have heard me gasp, or my teeth chattering, for they flung open the door. My Uncle - long, thin and terrifying with his black cloak, sallow skin and waxen, tallow-yellow fingers, snorted with laughter and had me brought in. I could have died of shame in my nightshift and bare feet.

He turned me this way and that, and looked me up and down as if he were buying a pony. He even took off my nightcap to look at my hair! For a moment I thought he might check my teeth. If he had, I would have bitten his yellow fingers.

He said, 'Yes, the girl's not too plain, but certainly not dazzling. She writes well and can hold her tongue? Modest, quiet and quick? She'll serve purpose. Can you keep secrets, child? Can you learn to hide in shadows?'

In a waking dream I heard my father listing my languages and accomplishments and the Duke saying he has found me a place as another of Queen Anne's Waiting Maids alongside my cousin Katherine. At COURT!

When Frances woke up she was hot with jealousy, 'You at Hampton Court Palace! Galumphing great you! At dances and banquets with all those elegant people? Your clothes will be all wrong. You don't know etiquette. You don't even know how to dance!'

I'm just thinking of the music, the hunting, the books, the cakes! And cousin Katherine.

It feels like a dream that comes with fever. I am to leave the day after my birthday. Oh dear heaven, can it be true?

My Birthday

We have been sewing and packing all day. Frances is still furious and full of annoying advice. I feel as if I have crossed to the other side of the mirror and am gazing on, separated from myself and all that is familiar. Caspian, Hunter, Lettyce, Frances, little Kate, stinking Robert, my dear parents… When will I see them again?

A list of birthday and parting presents - I, thirteen year old Matilda Marchmont - received:

 A long silver chain necklace from mother

 A silver horse charm, very like Caspian, from Frances.

 A mirror case of blue velvet embroidered by Frances with stars and moons, which she says is from Kate.

 A golden pear charm from father to hang on my chatelaine with my pomander.

 A lock of Caspian's mane entwined with myrtle from Lettyce.

 The family seal ring to wear on the chain. I can use it with sealing wax to seal my letters.

 A dug-up bone from Hunter - Robert's joke. Actually quite funny.

I am to have father's very own travelling trunk. It has a secret compartment that springs open and can only be unlocked by a tarnished silver key. I will hide you, most secret and precious journal, in it and wear the key on my new chain.

Mother has given me a big, dreary warning about not trusting my Uncle. She says he never signs letters in case people use them against him. She says he's never helped father in any way before. And didn't help Cousin Anne. 'Work hard and do as he says, but don't trust him too well, Matilda.' But he's sending me to court! Who cares about signed letters! I wish she'd stop fussing.

I must fly and help Frances let down the hems of my corduroy dress. I hope it will be fine enough for court.

Will the other Ladies at court have to see my darned underwear and holey stockings? I leave tomorrow. I leave FOR COURT tomorrow. I want to scream and jump up and down on my bed. I think I will.

A Raven

I can't stop shivering. I dreamt just now, I was in the orchard at night and a raven landed by me on a branch. Its feet trapped a strand of my hair, coiling it round my throat. In my pear tree was a lit-up window, where a girl, in a blood-red crown, paced backwards and forwards. The raven was pulling tight my hair, throttling me.

I must have screamed, for I woke up with Frances shaking me. My hair was wrapped round my throat where I'd tossed and turned. I jumped up to check my travelling trunk one last time. We leave at dawn for the long ride on Caspian to London. Mother forced me to break fast on pheasant and small beer and I feel sick to my stomach. I must fill my pomander with herbs to stop me puking.

I have just seen that Frances has slipped her best Christmas dress of russet velvet into my trunk. She loves that dress. It is her only good one.

What lies ahead? I can scarcely bear to say goodbye to my beloved family and my dear home. Journal, you are my only friend now.

Will Katherine like me? What will she be like? How on earth do I advance her with the King? Will she think me a bumpkin? Will she teach me what to say and how to do the dances? The King is wild for dances and masquerades. The King of England! I need the pot. I think I am going to throw up.

To London

My backside is so saddle-sore. Days and days of riding already. We cover about twelve miles a day as it rains and rains and there is so much mud, and sometimes snow. I feel more weary and excited and terrified with every mile closer to London and further from home.

I wonder what they're doing now? Frances will be sewing and rubbing my hare's brain lotion into Kate's gums. Mother and father will be fretting. I'll eat a bottled pear... Oh what will court be like?

We have stopped at an inn near the city gates.

London has more people than I could ever have imagined. A stew of stinking, thrilling streets full of pie-men and music-men and people with extraordinary animals and ragged beggars, all shouting for business.

Lettyce, who is travelling with me and Sykes, the manservant, is used to London and keeps pointing out things to me. She's showing off quite a bit, but I don't mind. She's my last link with home and will leave me all too soon.

When Lettyce turns back with Caspian and leaves me here I will have no friend but you, my journal. She says I can come into the city one night with her to see how dangerous and exciting it really is. She'll bring me a disguise. And maybe I'll meet Percy!

The sky was darkening and I could smell the river. A chill crept up on me as we neared an old bridge and my heart lurched. There was a row of faces, with decaying flesh and gouged-out eyes. Lettyce says airily, 'Oh yes, that's where traitors' heads go when there's an execution. They stick 'em on spikes after they cut them off, and leave 'em to rot. It's like a warning.'

Now the King is at Whitehall Palace but Lettyce says soon it may be Hampton Court or Greenwich. Her sister Pob works as a Royal laundry girl and tells her where the court is.

I had no idea that court really means this swarm of people that follows the King around. Thousands of courtiers and servants moving around from palace to palace with him.

We passed through the city gates and they said we were almost at Whitehall Palace.

I thought the Palace would a huge glittering castle - surrounded by gardens and fountains. But, from what I could make out in the darkness, it seems to be lots of houses within a ring of great walls.

Inside the gates it is a labyrinth of little cities within cities, with courtyards, and staircases leading down to the black river. I will never understand how it works. I was so tired and my backside so numb, my body seemed entirely separate from me – floating in the darkness, like the torches guiding us.

Inside the Palace

I am actually here. At court! My head aches with all the city sights and my trail through the palace.

A bad-tempered old lady, of about thirty, in a big headdress thing and a shiny black frock, who seems to be in charge of the lower Maids-of-Honour (if that is what I am), whisked me off. She told me to follow her and seemed very annoyed to have to deal with me at such an impossible time.

My legs were so chafed, I could barely keep up and I didn't have the energy to tell her that I hadn't caught her name. I'll call her The Hawk, as she has a beaky nose and shiny-cold eyes.

I caught glimpses of vivid rooms, flashing through gaps in velvet curtains, off endless corridors. Heavy smells of roast meats and perfumed puddings, made me faint with hunger.

Glittery people in extraordinary jewelled clothes, like human peacocks. Rooms and rooms of them, sitting at long tables feasting, or leaping about to wild, thrilling music.

There are portraits of the King in the long galleries, tall, broad-shouldered and handsome as a god with gleaming, red-gold hair. I shall be terrified when I actually see him. Though people say he is kind and funny.

At one point, a man in purple stockings staggered into the corridor. He bowed, pulled open some sort of domed object that covered his male parts and started pissing into a fireplace, right in front of us! The Hawk didn't seem at all astonished and just sniffed, a little disapprovingly. Surely women don't pee in fireplaces here?

At last we reached the Ladies' and Maids' quarters. They're nothing like the magnificent corridors upstairs. The Hawk told me I was allowed to go straight to bed tonight so I should be well rested to get up early tomorrow morning to be introduced to my duties.

She told me I am one of seventy Ladies-in-Waiting to Queen Anne. She brought some from Germany, of course. I have to share the youngest Maids' bedchamber with…it looks like… four other girls. Of course, I am to share this bed. They haven't come back from the feasting rooms yet. I suppose it won't be so different from sharing a bed with Frances.

The room is so cold. The Hawk reeled off something about how many bundles of firewood we are allowed and how many candles and jugs of beer and that we have all our meals with the King and Queen.

She told me what we were allowed to take away from the banquets and which were the lowliest Ladies and that I am a Maid-of-Honour, and the married ladies are called Ladies-In-Waiting and that some were Ladies of the Bedchamber, which is a better thing...

I was so tired all I wanted to know was when I'd get to see Katherine and where I could pee. I kept nodding and curtseying and mumbled something about, 'My cousin Katherine Howard.' She gave me an odd look and said, 'I daresay you shall meet her tomorrow.'

Maybe Katherine sleeps in this very room.

At last she said something about a jug of cold water for washing and pointed at a chamber pot.

When she left I collapsed onto the bed. I hope my bed-mate is nice and doesn't have stinking, clammy feet. Frances' feet are icy. I wonder if we are ever allowed to take baths here? At home Lettyce hauled heated water up for us and Robert gets in first, then Frances, then me.

They haven't brought my trunk in and I didn't dare ask The Hawk when I might get it. I pray it's not lost.

As I have no night-clothes yet, I have crept under the coverlet in my shift, clutching my journal and my chain. Caspian and the pear charm are pressing comfortingly into my flesh.

If only I was under the holey counterpane with Frances, listening to her snoring and Kate snuffling and father pacing below.

I thought I would sleep straight away but I cannot. Who will be sharing the room? Will they like me? What will they be wearing? Will they laugh at my shift in the morning? I can see my bed-mate's nightdress on the pillow. Embroidered.

I can just make out the shape of a huge headdress thing and a big, boned cage of some sort. How ever, where ever do you wear that? Or do you keep birds in it? And some tiny satin slippers embroidered with rosebuds. They look so thin and fine and high-heeled. Are they actually to wear, or are they ornaments?

It is so noisy here. At home all I hear are rooks and snores and shivering trees. Dance music is playing loudly. Fast, exciting rhythms with drums that make my heart quicken. I have heard of a dance called a volta and a pavane but I don't know which is which or what they are. Frances is right. I don't know anything about anything. I can hear leaping and the shaking of crockery and glasses. And laughing and drunken screams.

There's a strong smell in here of roasted meat, feet and perspiration. The rushes on the floor are full of discarded pieces of chicken-skin and mice scuttling. Upstairs, in those feasting rooms, fires were blazing, yet here it is so cold and smelly. The chamber pot's still full from the day.

And if gentlemen use the fireplaces…Lettyce's sister Pob told her that, at one great house, there is a communal 'place' where sixty four men and ladies can relieve themselves AT THE SAME TIME. I would die of shame.

A bell chimes one o'clock. Someone's coming down the passage.

Two girls giggling. Polished voices, 'Did you see the Mare's dung-brown frock! With her bum all flat! She looked even more like a farm horse tonight,' says one. The other laughs nastily, 'Shall I pull ze vagon now master, or into ze stable for ze night be comink?'

Candle out and pretend to be asleep. How will I ever fit in? Hide journal. They're coming in here.

Before Dawn

The girls are snoring away now. I've lit another candle.
I have to let my feelings out, journal, only friend. I could
barely understand what they were talking about.

'I'm caught in my wretched farthingale, Merry,' said one
of them.

'I've tied too many knots in my bum-roll ribbons, Meggy,'
replied the other, giggling like an idiot.

They tugged and fumbled off their layers of skirts. The
giggling one got into bed next to me, groaning. She's damp
and hot. She gave me a little shove and hissed over at the
other girl, 'Oh God, the new one's arrived. Hair looks like
a haystack!'

Don't be stupid Matilda. You longed for this adventure.
Now don't be a mouse. You never cry.

I am here at court in the most wondrous city in the world…
Peacocks dance, dukes piss in fireplaces, horses with satin
hooves pound my aching head as I swim down through
farthingale stars under my dampening pillow…hide
journal…to sleep…

My First Day

I have lived through more in one day here than in the whole of the rest of my life! I'm sitting up writing in bed again. I've told the other girls I'm listing all the new things they're teaching me about court!

As dawn broke I 'met' my new bed-mate. She was shoving me and pulling the coverlet off and, for a moment, I thought I had woken in my own bedroom with Frances. Until I saw her plump, cross face and heard her groaning about her sore head. She clambered over me and threw up into the overflowing chamber pot.

She hissed at me to get dressed quickly, 'Before Lady R arrives' who, I later gathered, must be The Hawk.

The puker is called Miggy, I think. Or Meggy. They all seem to have pet names beginning with M. I opened my trunk, which, thank heaven, had been brought in. I tried to quietly shake out Frances' crumpled, russet velvet gown. My fingers were trembling with cold and nerves. I wanted to conceal as much as possible from the other Maids in the room.

I tried to be quiet but, of course, I woke them - there is less privacy here even than at home. The other three girls peered over, looking with bleary, hopeful curiosity at me, in my baggy old shift.

One of them, I think she's called Merry or maybe Melly, a pretty, pointy-faced girl with a long neck, was the owner of the silk shoes. She came sliding over, smiling sweetly and fingered the edge of my velvet sleeve as I tried to pull Frances' dress on quickly, 'What lovely, unusual stuff. Is it from Paris?' she asked.

I was pleased, 'No, it's from Norfolk!' I said.

A loud snigger from her bed-mate. Frances' finest Christmas dress felt suddenly very shabby.

Merry or Melly pretended to be astonished, 'No! It can't be! It's so striking! But surely you've arrived from the French court. You have such…unique style!' she said.

The other girls spluttered behind their sheets and I blushed and dug my nails into my palms so that I would not cry. I tried to think of the perfect, snappish reply Lettyce would have for her.

She was delighted with her own wit, 'So aren't they wearing bum-rolls or farthingales or French hoods in Paris anymore?' she simpered. I pretended to be busy looking in my trunk.

She lifted the hem of my dress to look at my thick, woollen stockings, 'Nor silk stockings? I'll have to throw all mine out and order some from Norfolk. What would you call that lovely brown colour?'

She picked up my stout shoes and said, 'Will you be dancing in these for the Queen?' The other Merrys held their breath, loving the performance, 'Do you prefer a galliard or a volta or a bonbon?' I stammered out, 'A bonbon...But I don't really bother about dancing...or clothes.'

They all erupted and she exclaimed, 'That's not a dance, that's a French sugarplum! Didn't you eat them in Paris?' My face pin-pricked all over. Her little white hand started rummaging in the trunk.

I took the heavy lid and let it slam shut, narrowly missing trapping her fingers. She squealed in shock.

'Do you know my cousin Katherine Howard?' I asked coolly, and that shut her up for a bit. She shot a glance at her bed-mate, a plump girl, who was pulling on a transparent-looking shift, and turned on her heel.

They started un-plaiting each others' hair, which was wound into intricate shapes, and rolling it away from their temples. Whatever was I to do with mine? I could see now that all these things were very, very important here. Frances was right. Up? Down? I looked at my great, heavy, brown hood. And so did they.

They all have proper breasts and hips and must be at least fourteen. And their linen is so fine. No one said anything about breakfast and I definitely wasn't going to use the full chamber pot in front of them, though I was desperate to pee.

While they were busy plaiting and prattling, a fourth girl appeared from under the bedclothes and gave me a bleak smile. She was thin and pasty-faced, with lank hair. She pushed a less-full chamber pot over to me with her foot and started scrambling into her clothes. They were almost as plain as mine.

The pasty-faced girl – who doesn't have an M pet name - whispered that she is called Cecily. When the others, I'm just going to call them all The Merrys, were finally ready, I followed them down the corridor. They were giggling and holding hands. The giggling increased when they saw some boys, all dressed up in velvet and pearls, coming towards us.

The Merrys fell silent, then sort of fluffed themselves up, like roosting pigeons. The head Merry chirped out little scornful chirrups as the boys bowed and winked. Then, after we'd passed by, they erupted into a chorus of giggles again. It was all very strange. I cannot understand half the things they say or do. It seems as though everything is in a secret code I don't understand. A lot of the code seems to be to do with clothes.

It was all awful and, worst of all, it suddenly occurred to me: What if Katherine were as vile as the Merrys? Or worse?

They giggled through endless corridors, till we entered a series of grand, wood-panelled rooms. At the door to the last one they fell silent and bobbed angelic curtseys at The Hawk, who was waiting for us. It was a warm, tapestry-hung room, lit with lots of candles against the grey winter day. Dozens more women, dressed in complicated, terrifying clothes sat on low stools. They were sewing. Sewing! Perfect. All this way…for more sewing.

They looked me up and down a bit and one gave me a piece of linen and a needle but didn't tell me what to do with it. A door opened, on the other side of the room, and another group of women - dressed in elaborate, but ugly frocks and low, huge headdresses - entered, followed by lots of tiny dogs.

The sewing ladies greeted them stiffly and there was a frosty, bristling sort of atmosphere in the room. I gathered these must be Queen Anne's German Ladies

In the middle of them, not at all grandly in a procession sort of way, was the Queen herself. We all curtseyed. She is quite plain, with a flat, kind face. Her headdress is almost as ugly as mine - though it is made of rich fabrics - which made me like her. She even smiled and nodded at me. I do like her better than the English Ladies.

One of the Ladies barked at me, 'You, girl. Go and fetch the sewing silks,' I stammered that I didn't know where to go. As I stood up, my reels and thimble clattered to the floor. Sniggers all round. Then a beautiful girl in a green dress, with shining dark blonde hair, jumped up, took my hand and pulled me out of the room saying, 'I'll show her, Lady Sefton.'

When we were in the corridor she smiled, put her arm round my waist and whispered, 'You're my little cousin Matilda, aren't you? I'm Katherine. Uncle Norfolk said you were coming. I'm so glad.'

She has sea-green eyes and luminous skin and rosy, slightly-chapped lips. My eyes pricked with tears to hear kind words, but I sniffed them in.

She whisked me off to the older Ladies' room. It smelled better than ours. She made me sit on her bed and sat in front of me and held both my hands, smiling.

'You poor thing. It is strange at first in the Queen's rooms. And the girls can be cruel unless you stand up to them. You have to show them, but, you'll see, it's so much fun when you've got used to the boring stuff. Especially at night. And they're mostly mean to the German ladies – we call them Pumpkin Heads.'

At this I dissolved. She dabbed my eyes with her own handkerchief and a stream of sniffling woes came pouring out. 'It's just that I'm so hungry and the chamber pot was full of sick and I couldn't go anyway in front of those awful girls, and they laughed at my horrible shift and my underwear and my vile dress and my hood looks like a cabbage and I don't know what a bum-roll is or where I'm meant to sit or stand or when to curtsey or what I'm meant to do here… and I'm really bad at sewing…'

She laughed, but in a kind, teasing way, that made me laugh too, 'You're right, your dress is vile. And your hood does look like a cabbage. It would make me cry too! But it's not as bad as "ze Quveen's lehdees"'

'Melly Buxton can be a snake,' she went on, 'but don't worry, we'll soon sort her out. You should have seen her when she first came to court! Spots all over her face! I've lived in long-rooms with hundreds of girls, since I was a child and you just have to learn how to play the game. It's all about power!' she said. I nodded.

'And I'll tell you a secret…I never do any sewing. Life's too short for sewing.'

Within ten minutes the world seemed an entirely different place. Katherine fetched me a cup of sweet wine, a curranty bun and a gilded marchpane rabbit from last night's banquet. And, joy, she showed me a clean chamber pot, behind a curtain.

Then she was unlacing and pulling off the vile russet dress, 'You can borrow one of mine. Do you like this?' It was bottle green and silver, 'It will be beautiful with your hair. I'm going to ask our Uncle Norfolk to have you a court dress made. Pearly grey velvet, I think. With white fur. We can't have you letting down the Howards, can we?'

She piled under-linen on to my lap. I wasn't even sure what most of it was or how to begin to put it on. 'I'm sorry they're only old ones.' I'd never seen anything so soft and lovely.

She even added a pair of fine azure silk stockings, the colour of cloudless sky. 'They've got a hole in them, I'm afraid, but it's up high so you don't need to worry that it'll show when you're dancing.' Dancing! She said it so lightly. Me, dancing. In azure silk stockings!

'You and I are going to be such friends, Mattie.'

Katherine sat me in front of the mirror and looked at our faces side by side. Hers a luminous heart shape, mine a shadowy oval. She seemed pleased, but tilted her chin to inspect a tiny blemish on her perfect nose, 'I'm so spotty!' I told her I make Frances a lotion for spots.

She started brushing out my hair.

She smiled, 'You see. When you take off that cabbage hood and pull your hair back from your forehead and roll it, you're really pretty. And you must plait it at night,' she said.

Her fingers started to fly, like Melly's, making long twirly ropes of hair. I began to look - well, I wouldn't say pretty but, I began to look…like one of them, 'You just need a French hood.'

'I don't have so many things myself yet. But maybe one day soon…I shall. There are so many gorgeous rich boys at court.' She smiled a knowing, lop-sided smile and her eyes flashed. I asked her if the King was very handsome and she looked at me strangely. I'm not sure why.

'I can see I'm going to have to teach you everything.' Then my education truly began.

Bit by bit the code of court clothes started to come clear… Katherine started to dress me in her underwear and the green and silver court dress.

You have to wear a fine cotton shift underneath everything. You can change it and have it washed as often as you can afford. You sweat into it, so it stops your expensive frock from getting stained.

Katherine says she makes an effort to smell nice at dances and banquets, 'Whenever men might smell you'. It never occurred to me to think how I'd smell to men – Robert is always so stinky. But it seems to be something to do with power again. She'll like my perfumed waters and the vinegar and camomile I sponge under my arms. I will make her some tomorrow.

First on over the shift goes the farthingale. It makes your hips stick out in a square. It's made of sticks which I think are willow canes. When I saw how it made me look – like a bird in a cage – I felt like a real courtier. But Katherine says lots of fashionable French ladies don't wear them any more and nor does she.

She told me, 'You're much freer to dance without one and they make you look as though you don't want to be touched.' Personally, I don't want to be touched. But I think I might quite like to be fashionable.

A bum-roll gives a softer shape to your behind and makes your stomach look more flat. It's a big pad of cloth tied on over your bum. She's lent me a linen one.

The court dress has lots of parts, 'So you can make it seem like you have more than one...' There are different pairs of sleeves to tie on with laces, to the bodice. And material to puff through them in patterned slits.

It has a low, daring French neckline – thankfully worn over the shift to cover my chest. Katherine leaves hers bare. She says it makes people notice you. You wrap long pieces of cloth round your breasts and make them stand up a bit. I would hate that. Anyway, luckily I don't really have any yet.

Katherine seems very proud of her breasts though. She does exercises to make them bigger.

'Our cousin Anne Boleyn brought French styles over here and now some of the fashionable maids, like me, and actually mostly they copied me...are wearing French things again. They make you look gorgeous.'

She admired my chain and charms. Luckily she didn't notice the key.

The stomacher that holds your breasts in place, is really tight and flattens your belly. Katherine laced it up to give me a tiny waist. It was so tight I felt ill and had to breathe in small breaths. I couldn't believe it was on right.

I winced and she said, 'Do you want to look like a German! You can put the cabbage back on and join the Pumpkin Heads if you want…' She pulled me into the best position to see myself in the small mirror.

Now my shape looked almost like hers. Not as perfect of course. And she is fifteen. But easily as good as any of the Merrys. We shifted around, on and off the beds, to see as much of ourselves as we could in the small, silvered mirror. Katherine said, 'The Queen has a huge mirror – you'll see it this evening when we get her ready. You can see your whole length in it. I love it.' For the first time, I could see why people might be interested in clothes. They change you.

We looked at ourselves critically. She grabbed my hips and said, 'You have to watch how many syllabubs and bonbons you eat. It's very important to be slender at court.'

I had never given a thought to it before but I can see it must be important here. And I had been so looking forward to all the desserts.

The final thing was the French hood. You wear it pushed right back to show your hair, not like my clumpy English one or the German pumpkins. It has gold lace round the edge. Katherine says she wants to get one with billiments one day, which are jewel-encrusted edges.

She has the very latest one, which she wears so far back it needs a strap to hold it on under her chin, so you can see her smooth hair. It has a fine black lace veil that swishes over her shoulders. Katherine doesn't put her hair into a net like the other girls, she leaves it tumbling down her back.

'It really makes boys notice you,' she said. I don't know why you'd want that. I hope no one notices me tonight.

I tied my chain girdle around my waist and Katherine sniffed my pomander of herbs from home. I told her I can make lots of tinctures like headache remedies and sleeping draughts. I could see she was interested. 'What about skin whiteners and lip paint?'

She dabbed a bit of white powdery stuff from a tiny pot, onto my face. When I looked at myself in the mirror I was utterly transformed. I felt a wing-flap of excitement in my chest. We stood side by side looking in the glass. Two fashionable maids of court!

But when I asked her if there were lots of lovely books at court, Katherine laughed as if I'd said something outrageous, 'Girls don't need to say things like that! Especially don't ever say them to men. I can see I need to teach you everything!'

I think I flushed and said I wished she would teach me everything – like what I'm meant to do for Queen Anne for a start.

'Oh I wouldn't worry too much about all that!' she laughed. 'That's the boring part. Just do what I do. Come on, we better fly back now or Lady R. will be after us.'

'I call her The Hawk,' I said cautiously. Her peal of laughter came like a benediction and she grabbed my hand and pulled me down the corridor.

When the Merrys saw me they didn't recognise me at first. They looked respectful but suspicious. Then I saw Katherine whisper something to one of them. There is an odd uncertainty in the way they regard Katherine. I am not sure what it is. But she has some sort of power. She's beautiful and lively and fashionable, of course, and everybody wants to be like her or have her like them and laugh at their jokes. But there's something else too.

They all call her Kitty. Kitty Howard. But I think Katherine is a beautiful name and I shall always call her that.

When the Merrys and I went to our room to get ready for the evening they were much less nasty. They sat on my bed and admired the green gown and the hood. Then they jumped up on their beds, shouting 'Veil fight! Veil fight!' and we started throwing our veils at each other, until we heard The Hawk's heels clicking down the hall.

As I put the new under-linen on top of my travelling chest, I caught the head Merry eyeing the blue stockings enviously.

Later, we were called to the Queen's rooms and one of the lesser Merrys linked arms with me. We ran through all eight rooms to the Queen's privy chamber to help prepare her for the banquet tonight.

Sweating servants brought in buckets of heated water. All we seemed to have to do was stand around holding things and passing them to the more important Ladies.

I had to hold a sheet then pass it up the line to one of the other Maids to give to a Lady who was allowed to dry the Queen after her bath. Katherine gave me little encouraging looks. Then I got to pass a silver hairbrush to a Maid, who passed it to a Lady, who passed it to a Lady who was allowed to brush royal hair.

When I asked the Merrys what I would have to do at the banquet, they laughed and one said, 'It's a long meal tonight, with some boring ambassadors. The Queen'll be at table for hours…You're doing the very important duty…It's a special honour for new girls. We all had to do it.' Then they laughed again.

Under the Table

I soon found out what the 'Very important duty' was. Well,
I guessed it wasn't going to be anything good…

I didn't get to see more than courtiers' legs all evening.
On important occasions, i.e. very long ones, the Queen isn't
allowed to leave the table if she needs to pee. She'd have
to be cut out of her farthingale anyway, if she did.

So two younger Maids-of-Honour need to stay under the
table and, when she gives the signal, hold this large pot
thing under her and pull apart her kirtle for her to pee into
and then whip the pot out again. Then one of us passes it
discreetly to a servant to empty and gets another pot ready
for the next signal.

The other girl, inevitably, was Cecily, from our room. Her
dress was almost as vile as my old one, poor thing. She
seemed a bit in awe of me now she knew I was Katherine's
cousin and one of The Howards. She asked me shyly if I
liked reading, which surprised me, and said she knows how
to get hold of books. We giggled when the Queen started
talking loudly to mask the sound of her pee spurting into
the metal pot.

I was glad not to be on show tonight, having to perform, though it was frustrating hearing only muffled bits of the singers and not being able to see the funny jester – the King's Fool.

But I enjoyed studying the ladies' jewelled shoes and the rainbow of silk stockings and trying to work out their rank by their feet. Cecily pointed out who was wearing dirty linen and the strange signals one or two of the lords and ladies gave each other under the table. I recognized Katherine's yellow silk shoes and saw a boy's hand drop a note onto her lap.

I still have not seen the King. But his legs looked long and enormous under the table.

His great, square-toed shoes were studded with amethysts and his laugh was deep and magnificent.

Katherine slid us a plate of almond sweetmeats and some wine under the table

At last Cecily and I were released, for the Queen wanted to go to bed – before the dancing, much to Katherine's despair.

I followed her to help prepare the Queen for bed. We spent ages taking off all the layers which we had put on her that evening. Katherine and I nearly had a giggling fit at the odd German rolls of puddingy padding.

The older ladies put her nightgown over her head and I
held a comb while they brushed out her hair and plaited it
up prettily under her nightcap. Then we all knelt and said
prayers with the Queen's priest. It seems so funny, that great
number of us, dressing and undressing one small twenty-
four year old woman.

I would hate to be a Queen and have everyone fussing
over me and looking at me naked and to have no privacy
or peace.

Katherine says she would love to have all those women
obeying her every whim. She would look much better in the
Queen's rubies.

I had to leave before the King came, in thank goodness, as
I am still new. I was exhausted and relieved not to have had
to dance and not to have dropped a brush and that I was
wearing the right hood. I felt my day had been quite
a success.

On our way back to the Maids' rooms I saw an open
doorway. A room full of beautifully bound books, piled
on glossy tables. I long to go in there. I will ask Cecily
tomorrow if it is allowed.

Merry, the snake, took my arm, 'How was your evening? I hope you had a nice view and didn't get too wet,' she said. I hesitated for a moment and glanced at Katherine. Then I said something I'm not proud of, 'Well at least I had Cecily for company. Yawn. No need for a sleeping powder now.' Katherine let out her peal of laughter, followed by the other girls.

Cecily slipped out of the shadows nearby and walked on quickly ahead. I felt a prickly flush of shame. But then Katherine linked arms with me and said, 'Come on Mattie…' and we ran back to the Maids' rooms.

What a first day. Sitting up in the lumpy bed, a wave laps me – it feels like a sickness until I recognise it. Missing home. But then I feel a flutter of excitement again. I, Matilda Marchmont, am here. I am here at court with Katherine. The most interesting girl, in the most interesting place in the world, is my friend. I am a Mattie!

I must be careful to lock this away in the compartment when the Merrys are asleep, in case they decide to snoop at my 'list of court rules'.

I See The King

I have seen the King! I was so surprised, I nearly shrieked.
He is not quite like I imagined him. Not really like all the
portraits of the young golden hero. He is old! Katherine
says he is forty-eight. He is very tall – a full six feet four, and
he is wide. He must be four feet across. He has great broad
shoulders and you can see he is strong and brave and witty.

He was magnificently dressed, in pearl-encrusted velvet,
with his legs in silver tights. He was strung with jewelled
chains and his fingers clustered with rings. There is an air
of tremendous power about him, which is almost magical.
Grave councillors and handsome boys all seems to flutter
about him, like moths around a giant flame. And he makes
them laugh a great deal.

I curtseyed low, looking at the ground as he came past and
whispered, 'Majesty', like Katherine did. He smiled at we
younger girls and his eyes twinkled!

The first part of this afternoon was spent pretend-sewing,
which means gossiping by the fire in the Queen's rooms.
Through the window, we could see the King getting onto
the royal barge from the pier, with his men. Light sparked
off his jewelled cloak through the fog.

Katherine pulled me out into one of the smaller rooms saying, 'Your next lesson, Mattie. Dancing. No protests', She knew I'd been dreading this.

There was a fire and Katherine had even arranged a lute player. Though I wished the Merrys hadn't come in to watch. First she taught me a pavane, which is slow and strutty and not too complicated. I felt quite pleased I could manage it, with Katherine guiding my feet and hands. Even with the Merrys gawping at me.

Then she showed me a volta, which is fast and passionate. She's thrilling to watch. I was dizzy and damp, as though I'd been galloping on Caspian. I loved it. Katherine laughed, but in an encouraging way. When I fell over, catching my heel in my kirtle, which is too long for me, all the Merrys sniggered.

In a break in the music I said, 'Katherine, didn't you tell me about a girl who thought a galliard was a ship, when she first came to court?' Merry number three flushed and it shut them all up for a bit. Katherine roared with laughter.

After that we played some card games with the Queen at lots of little tables. I didn't know how to play those either. The Queen, who loves cards, was very kind and patient. The Pumpkin Heads cheer up a lot when they're playing cards.

Then we all clustered in to dress the Queen for another banquet. My first banquet sitting at table. No pissing duty for me. Though poor Cecily is doing it again. I think they always make her do it. She gave me a resigned smile, but she didn't seem envious of me being with the Merrys.

The food. I have never seen such wonders. Our family could have lived for months on this one meal. The King sat on an enormous throne draped with cloth of gold. Servants kneel down to serve him and offer him golden bowls to wash his fingers. He only eats after his food-taster has checked for poison, which he really fears. There might be Italian poison rings anywhere.

Everyone is terribly keen to please him, or, rather, terrified of displeasing him, and all the women smile prettily at him, except Queen Anne, who doesn't really do that sort of thing. It is very important at court to learn how to be charming. It gives you power.

There were choices of at least thirty dishes in each course. There were roasted swans and larks and tiny sparrows and blackbirds baked in shiny pies called coffins. There were peacocks, served as if still alive, in their shimmering feathers, but they've been roasted with plums and stuffed back inside the gorgeous body. Some oysters with apricots made me feel a bit sick so I spat them out into my hand.

The King's fingers flashed with rubies as he ate dish after dish.

The music was wonderful – there were lute players and drummers and all sorts of new songs. Many of them composed by the King.

The puddings were like one of Kate's dreams. All sorts of creatures carved out of pink and green marchpane, rose-water creams studded with crystallised violets, towers of gleaming candied quinces.

Katherine gave me a sharp look when she saw me try two puddings – a syllabub and a lilac custard. I watched her eat as though the food were hardly important at all. She does this quite loud little laugh, narrowing her green eyes, like a cat, wrinkling her nose and tossing her hair. I saw lots of boys glancing at her. She is by far the prettiest girl in the room.

People came in and out between courses. Katherine says some really greedy courtiers leave to puke up, so that they can eat more.

When I left to pee, a servant approached me in the corridor, wearing the Howard crest, and passed me a rolled up note. I knew it must be from my Uncle. Unsigned, like Mother said. Well it's for security reasons and that's important at court. She doesn't understand.

The note said:

'I hope you have spoken to your cousin of the matter in hand. Remember why you are here. I have sent your father some venison from my estates and some velvet bed hangings and may send a fine horse. Destroy this.'

I felt a sickening lurch to the stomach, like falling out of a tree. Taste of oysters coming back up into my mouth. I had almost forgotten my secret. I am here to serve my family.

After the meal the King sang one of his own songs. He is a gigantic presence. Not just because of his size.

People applauded wildly. The German Ladies didn't though. They don't really understand our etiquette at court. The most important thing is that you can't show what you're really feeling. Thank goodness I have Katherine to copy. And thank goodness I had her clothes on.

Then there was a masque – a sort of play, with music where people posed about in costumes, against some curtains painted to look like sky. Katherine says she and the Merrys are going to perform in front of the whole court in a really big masque before Lent and have gorgeous costumes and masks made. She said she's going to get me into it too.

I sat frozen to my chair when the ladies began to dance. It was a pavane. Horrors, they were joined by a group of men, and the lines and patterns seemed very elaborate. Much more so than those we'd learnt in the Queen's rooms. I watched Katherine turn and walk and join hands gracefully. Not like poor Queen Anne in her great pumpkin hood.

Katherine was entrancing. She smiled at one handsome young man after another, swishing to and fro in her dusky pink gown and her yellow shoes. She must not have realised that she was showing quite a lot of her rose-coloured stockings.

The King loves watching the dancing and was apparently the best dancer in Christendom, when he was younger. As Katherine wove in and out of the dance, like a pink satin ribbon through the braid of young men, I felt very aware of Uncle's note in my pocket.

The King's Knight-of-the-Bed-Chamber, Thomas Culpepper, with brown curly hair and eyes like crystallized violets on a syllabub, is a very good dancer. He's just come back to court after a jousting accident and is the King's favourite. All the Merrys swoon over him.

He slid smoothly amongst the women, like mercury. Katherine took his hand and then rejoined the line. His bright eyes lingered on her.

I was so grateful just to be able to sit and watch. How could the playhouse be more exciting than this! I think Queen Anne just wanted to watch too. She is quite shy, like me. I couldn't quite shake off the sick, lurching feeling that Uncle's note had given me though.

Suddenly Katherine pulled me up to dance. The room swirled and turned and re-formed as she laughed and mouthed instructions. I think I only turned the wrong way once. Or twice.

I'm writing in bed, my head is spinning from the wine and the music. My first banquet and my first dance. I am here. My name is Matilda Marchmont and I have eaten roast peacock and cygnets and whole menageries of marchpane and danced in front of the King and Queen of England. I wish I could tell Lettyce.

I haven't thought about Lettyce or Frances all day. I am heartless. Or maybe I'm brave. I think of the fine things Uncle has sent home. Things I have earned for them all. How pleased mother must be to have the velvet bed hangings. How proud of me they will be and how sophisticated they will find me after this great adventure.

If I can but persuade Katherine to enchant the King...I must put my journal beneath my pillow and sleep, galloping Caspian through a forest of jewelled giants and violet-eyed courtiers and Katherine's golden, leaf-strewn hair...

I Make Some Progress

I had my chance after breakfast. Katherine and I were walking in the frosty courtyards. There are no gardens here at Whitehall, but it is good for secret conversations.

We were meant to be grooming one of the little dogs. I took a breath and said, 'I heard the King doesn't care for Queen Anne…'

Katherine's eyes lit up. She loves gossip. I went on, 'I've heard he doesn't like her looks…or her smell. They say he blames Thomas Cromwell, his advisor – you know – the sallow one at dinner who always wears black…'

She nodded. I put the little dog on the rim of a frozen fountain and started brushing it. Ridiculous little thing. It's not what I would call a dog.

She giggled, 'Yes…Cromwell had a portrait of her painted by some famous painter – Hans something – so the King could see what she looked like, before he said he'd marry her. Well now he says it made her look much prettier than she is and that she looks like a horse.'

'Looks do seem to be very important to the King.' I said. She laughed, 'They're important to everyone! They're the most important thing in the world! You are a child sometimes Mattie. One can tell you grew up in the country!'

I didn't like that much! But I thought I was working up quite well to sowing a seed for Uncle's plan. So I buried my face in the shivering dog and said, 'Wouldn't it be a great thing for the King if he could marry again for love? Someone lovely and beautiful. He couldn't take his eyes off you last night when you were dancing in your rose frock.'

Katherine flushed, surprised. She expected to be admired of course, but I don't think it had entered her head to think of replacing the Queen.

The idea intrigued her, 'Imagine being Queen – all the things I'd have…But he's so ancient. I'm looking for a young man to marry. A handsome rich one, of course.' She laughed, as though she were mocking herself, but really she meant it.

'You'd be so good at performing all the royal ceremonies though…' I prompted.

Her eyes began to shine. 'It would be exciting to make the King fall in love with me - the most powerful man in the world. And to make him happy. And to be a really regal Queen for the people. One who knows how to dress…'

I nodded. 'Yes, and you'd be so good at presiding over the jousting and planning the masques. And you'd wear the crown with such elegance at pageants, and have all those courtiers vying for your favours…Think how you'd look in the rubies!'

I could tell she was thinking about it seriously…and was maybe thinking I wasn't such a childish country bumpkin after all. Imagine if I could always advise her. How helpful I'd be. How good for the Howards. How good for the people and the country.

Then The Hawk appeared, so we looked busy with the silly dog.

A Compliment

This afternoon we were in the Queen's chamber, folding shawls. Katherine stood in front of the big mirror. She dropped into a deep curtsey and looked up, biting her lips a little, and murmured breathlessly, 'Your Majesty', as though the King were there.

'I like to practise how I'm going to do things,' she said, 'It's important to know how you look to the man you want to admire you. That's how women have power, you know.'

I never think of things like that, but I must learn to. Although I think it only works for pretty people.

An hour later, a page came to say that the King was coming to the Queen's rooms to visit. Everyone rushed around, fluttering like mad, fetching tables and musicians and drinks. Katherine found her spot and whispered in my ear, 'I think I will stand against this green tapestry. It flatters my complexion.'

The King arrived, magnificent with huge velvet shoulders, slashed and puffed with silk, surrounded by a flock of men. He said he'd like to watch us dance.

The musicians were called up for a galliard. Katherine
threw a few modest looks at the King as she skipped up
the room. When we'd finished he stood up and walked
along the line of ladies. He stopped right in front of us
and my heart turned over. He complimented Katherine
on her graceful turns. She drifted into her deep curtsey
and breathless, 'Your Majesty'. Her eyes glinted after he'd
left. I felt quietly triumphant.

I wrote a note on a piece of the Queen's paper to Uncle.
I told him about the dancing and the compliment and how
much clever encouragement I'd given Katherine. I sanded
it and gave it to his servant. It felt strange, but important
and good, to know I am helping both my best friend and
my family.

Presents

Later this afternoon, when we were re-doing our hair in Katherine's room, a servant arrived. He brought a chest containing two new gowns for Katherine. One with silver embroidery and an azure silk kirtle. And a new hood with pearls around the edge, instead of just lace, 'Billiments!' Katherine squealed, 'I love Uncle!'

She was so thrilled with the hood that she gave me her other one.

Underneath, we found the court dress that Katherine had Uncle order for me. It is the most beautiful thing I have ever seen. Designed by Katherine – silvery grey velvet with full sleeves, lined with white fur and a kirtle of plum silk and a perfect tight stomacher. And a pair of grey velvet dancing shoes. And chopines to tie on the shoes when I go out, so I can walk on little wooden platforms above the mud. And undershifts. And a pretty night cap.

Katherine put on her new gown and helped me put on my bum-roll and tie my stomacher really tight.

We jumped on the bed and wriggled about to try and see ourselves in the small mirror. She saw me admiring myself for the first time and said, 'You look like a real Maid-of Honour now, not a dairy maid,' as she swiped me with a pillow and I swiped back with another. We started laughing and coughing so hysterically in the flurry of goose feathers that I thought I might wet myself.

Cecily ran past us, in the corridor with a pile of embroidery silks and looked longingly in. Katherine stuck out her tongue and Cecily blushed and looked away, a little afraid. We collapsed, laughing on the bed in our new finery, covered in a snow-drift of feathers

Then another servant arrived. One of the King's men. He had a little box for Katherine. A silver necklace. From the King.

We looked at each other, excited. Our new hoods still floured with feathers. We were almost frightened. Still and quiet.

I saw her smile in the misted mirror as I fastened the necklace. We clasped hands and did a little dance step, perfectly, sinuously in time with each other. We two impoverished Howards suddenly felt like the most powerful girls at court.

Another Palace

An exhausting day packing everything up to move to Hampton Court Palace. I was so excited at the thought of seeing it at last! So many things had to go with us – mirrors and the best carpets and cushions from the Queen's rooms. All her wardrobe, in trunk after trunk, and the dogs and bed linen, and gold plates and musical instruments. Even the King's great bed was trundled onto carts.

We rode out of the gates of Whitehall Palace in a great procession and into the narrow streets. I had a fat small horse, not like lovely Caspian, and I had to wear my old riding dress again. I didn't want to spatter my court dress with filth from the streets…But it looked fine with my new plum cloak over it .

They'll start clearing the Palace now – sweeping out the rushes full of food and sprinkling new ones on the floors with lavender and cleaning the pissing places.

The whole city was out to look at the new Queen. Poor Queen Anne. Katherine was so confident. She swished her head from side to side as though everyone were here to look at her, not the Queen. Well she did look much more magnificent than the Queen. Of course people love looking at her. She's really excited about the masque. We're going to practise for hours. I still had to remind myself it was real. That I, Matilda Marchmont, was riding in the royal cavalcade to Hampton Court Palace.

The city stank of gutters and chamber pots tipped out of windows. Amidst the crowd, there were pedlars, street entertainers and book-sellers. People shouted greetings to the royal party over the noise of the hooves. The King waved from his white stallion, glittering with diamonds. Thomas Culpepper was riding alongside him. They dazzled. I saw Thomas glancing at Katherine several times as we snaked through the town. It made me think, uneasily, of Uncle's warnings.

We started to ride along the riverbank and the air became fresher. Reflections of clouds and boats shivered on the dark water of the river. The Thames is like a little city itself. It teems with merchants' barges and wherries, which Lettyce had told me are the big boats that common people pack into.

We left the chill river and I felt a pang as I started to smell the damp grass and see early buds on the horse-chestnut trees. Wet sheep huddling. I wonder if Lettyce will really come one day?

We passed through a village where a monastery was being knocked down. It was being made into a house for one of the King's councillors. Statues of saints were being thrown onto a pile, their chipped faces looked sorrowful. The medicinal herb garden was being dug over. I glanced at Katherine, to see if she were shocked too, but she was looking at Meggy's new riding boots.

'Wait till you see what wonderful hunting there is at Hampton Court, Mattie,' Katherine said. Great packs of hunting dogs have travelled with us. Hunting's one of the King's passions. No one said anything about the beautiful saints piling up. The King's fool cantered out and started up some silly song.

Still, we provided a wonderful pageant for the villagers, who cheered Queen Anne and I am happy for her. I think she was nervous. The King waved and beamed about him, glittering like a god.

At last, up ahead, I glimpsed a dash of scarlet. Hampton Court Palace itself. And, oh it is beautiful. It is really like a Palace. Enormous and graceful and unimaginable. It is bright red brick with sparkling white arches. We rode through a high stone gateway, down a wide drive and into a gracious courtyard. There are endless elegant gardens here, laced with alleys and rainbows of flowers and fountains, leading down to the river.

Hundreds of servants lined up, in order of rank, to greet the King and Queen. And the huge household moved in – about eight hundred of us - with all the furnishings and tapestries and dogs. I was worried my trunk might be lost in all the thousands of finer ones, with my new grey dress and sleeves, and my journal, locked safely in the secret compartment, but luckily it has arrived safely.

In the Maids' room here eight of us share, so I will be with Katherine. Katherine flung herself onto the best bed by the window with the heaviest coverlet, 'Now, who shall I choose to share with?' She teased, glancing from one to another of us, resting on poor Cecily for a moment, before, of course, choosing me.

I can hardly believe I am sharing a bed with Katherine. We stayed awake whispering and giggling half the night. I said we'd have so much fun plotting and planning our secret, 'her' plan to dazzle the King. Just as I wanted, she fully believes it's her idea now.

It is dawn and I'm the only one awake, sitting up scribbling, with my cloak round my shoulders. I woke to hear rooks cawing round the towers. Real birds, not the river gulls at Whitehall, and light through trees, and gardens wet with dew. I found my eyes full of tears. But I wouldn't want dull old Frances lying asleep beside me instead of Katherine with her yellow hair spread on the pillow.

Katherine who makes everything exciting and sparkling and new.

Uncle will expect a report soon. I must impress him with some concrete progress. Katherine must really stand out at the masque on Tuesday night. Once it is Lent all the festivities and dancing will stop until Easter. Katherine says she's dreading Lent as it is really boring.

But a masque! With costumes and disguises and lines of poetry to say and dance steps to learn and masks to wear. I can do a pavane, a galliard and a volta perfectly now. I think.

Rehearsals

Katherine has made detailed plans for our hair: Flowing, with little braids at the front, laced with ribbon and white flowers and leaves, 'To give us a bridal, innocent sort of look,' she said.

We were practising a song for the masque, when a note arrived from Uncle asking me to meet him in one of the rose gardens.

His yellow face was pinched and stern, 'So, how does it progress? What are you proposing to do next?'

I told him how delightful Katherine is going to be at the masque, 'Well she must dazzle him before Lent. Mind that she does, child. I shall be there of course. Watching.'

He also warned me again about boyfriends, 'She must be pure as snow. No one in the past and no flirtations now. Is there anyone she looks at?' I thought of Thomas Culpepper and how her face lights up a little when he's near.

'No, no one, Uncle,' I said innocently. I would never betray Katherine. But I will warn her she must stay away from Thomas now. I can give her good advice as her truest friend. I can only imagine what those stupid Merrys would advise her to do! Uncle's eyes shine black in his tallow face, 'She must be bold. Use those cunning wiles women employ. I have sent your father a horse. And new livery.'

I ran back to find Katherine trying on her half-finished masque dress. She looked like a mermaid against the dark panelled walls, 'Not cut too low, is it?' she asked delightedly. That would make her stand out. But I needed something more.

Uncle had sent us the material for the dresses. Mine is green, watery silk, with lacing – like a medieval princess. I try on my silk mask and look in the glass. It lines my eyes with silver and makes me look like a cat and utterly unlike myself. Not like a 'child' at all.

An Idea

Since dawn, there has been hammering and scenery-painting and musicians practising and dressmakers bustling.

I slipped in to watch, from behind a curtain, as the scene men rehearsed with the musicians. As the lute players plucked faster and faster, there was a great bang and an explosion of sparks shot into the air at the front of the stage. I shrieked, thinking a cannon had gone off. The men found me and laughed. They explained that it was something called fireworks, for the end of the masque. A surprise for the King.

I asked the lute players what part of the music they'd be playing when the explosions began.

I knew what I was going to do.

Masque

Our finished dresses arrived and I lifted the watery silk out of its wrappings. When I saw my shimmering self, bodice tightly laced with lavender ribbons, I felt transformed. Brave. So far away from the girl in the pear tree.

Katherine looked wonderful with her flower-strewn hair and silver dress. When she tied on her mask she looked extraordinary but I looked touched by magic too. I looked powerful. I swished my hair to check my headdress and felt just like Katherine. The Merrys raced in to see us and gasped. They clustered round us like petals. Kitty and Mattie. The Howard girls.

Everyone wanted to be like us. To be with us. Even just to trail along after us. Cecily looked at me from her bed in the Maids' room. She was reading and not taking part in the masque, of course. She smiled and said I looked like Melissande, in the old legend. Katherine snorted.

She took my hand and we ran giggling down the corridor. We almost ran into a man in a glittering silver mask. It was Thomas Culpepper. He pretended not to recognise us in our disguises, but of course he did. He did a special bow for Katherine and she tossed her hair. I shall have to watch him. The audience were already in their seats, flanking the King's golden throne. He looked restless and I could see his servants were anxious lest they do something wrong. We stood behind the curtain and the musicians began to play. My heart was beating painfully but I could feel Katherine's was too. She squeezed my hand and it began.

At first, I was dazzled by the hundreds of candles and the scenery with its painted stars and flames, but I caught up and we all danced forwards, scattering petals. Thanks to all Katherine's practising it was going perfectly. Well almost…Miggy did tread on my train and I almost set light to Meggy's plait in the candle dance, but neither of those were accidents.

The music started to build to its final frenzy and we began to form the Tudor rose shape at the centre of the stage for the finale…I watched the lute players, counted time and made my move. I took a deep breath and shoved Katherine hard, right to the front of the stage so that all the fireworks would explode right around her. She was lit up - her silver dress and burnished hair a constellation of stars.

The thunder of applause was all for her. She knew all eyes were on her. Most importantly, the King's. I could almost feel my Uncle's tarry black eyes shine with approval.

The King came over to congratulate the performers and we sank into curtseys. He took Katherine's chin in his hand and raised her face and said something I couldn't hear. He was smiling now. I think he loves her already. I glanced over at Uncle. He gave me a slight nod.

After the King had gone back to the table to eat, Katherine
pulled me into the shadows. Her face was lit up. I was dying
to hear what the King had said. She was all in a spin, drunk
on the King's admiration, but there was something else too.
Thomas Culpepper had asked her to meet him in the knot
garden tomorrow, 'Shall I send him an answer, Matilda?'
I thought of my Uncle and she saw my expression and
taunted me that she'd get Melly to take a message if I was
too scared.

Well yes, of course I was afraid. This wouldn't help with
the King. She mustn't get sidetracked when it was starting
so well. How much trouble would I get into with Uncle?
He'd send me home in disgrace, for sure, and I'd never see
Katherine again.

What does Uncle know about girls of our age though?
I couldn't let Melly become her confidante. And I was
wearing my mask. I made a quick decision. I waited till
we were in line for a galliard, then with one eye on Uncle's
dour watchful face in the corner, I saw him turn away for
a cup of wine. Heart beating, I danced casually towards
Thomas Culpepper and whispered into his ear.

Another Secret

This morning, just as I was writing a note to my Uncle about what the King had said to Katherine, something about her being a 'Perfect rose without a thorn', a page came in carrying a gilded box. Katherine's eyes lit up. We knew it was from the King.

She unfurled a roll of golden cloth which will make a wonderful gown for Easter. And a silver hand-mirror with a curly handle like a skein of cobwebs.

She was really excited. So I warned her that she had to be honest with the King if she wanted more presents. And more power. I told her, 'He would want to be absolutely your first love, you know.'

'Do you think maybe I shouldn't meet Thomas Culpepper in the garden today then?' she asked. I nodded as though this was a wise idea. I didn't tell her that was exactly what I had already whispered to him last night at the masque.

Then she asked me if I could keep a secret. I am beginning to feel quite good at keeping secrets. She took me to the window seat and drew a curtain round us.

Then she told me a very dangerous thing. 'Two years ago – there was this boy,' she whispered, '...at my grandmother's house. He was called Francis Dereham. In the long rooms... he used to come to the midnight feasts, to see me. He was in love with me and he sort of even pretended to marry me...But I was only thirteen. Just a child, really...' she said.

I am only thirteen myself, but people seem to expect a lot of me if I am still 'just a child'. Though for, 'a child', I feel I am coming on fast to the ways of court.

I grasped her hands and looked her firmly in the eye and told her she mustn't ever, ever, ever mention this to anyone. Especially not to Uncle or the King...or even the Merrys. Not to anyone. She could lose everything.

'I'll never talk about him again. I'll completely forget it ever happened. But how could the King marry me if he's married to the Queen? I don't understand...'

I reminded her of how he met his last two wives before Queen Anne. That our cousin Anne was Lady-in-Waiting to Catherine, his first wife. Then he fell in love with Anne. Then Jane Seymour was Lady-in-Waiting to Anne, his second wife, when he fell in love with her.

Katherine laughed, 'And now I'm Lady-in-Waiting to his fourth wife…He met them in the Queen's rooms, fell in love with them and…'

I nodded and said, '…then he put them on the throne. So why not you?'

Katherine's eyes glittered, 'Do you really think I could do it?'

I gave the note to Uncle's man and felt I had done a good morning's work.

I had both warned and encouraged Katherine and I know a secret my Uncle doesn't know. And I had already stopped her seeing Thomas, and made her think it was her own idea. I think I am beginning to understand how court life works now. I have been watching Thomas Cromwell. How he never shows his feelings on his face, but is always calmly planning his next move. As Uncle says, 'Keep a clear head and stay in the shadows.'

Power ✿

On the way back to the Queen's rooms one of the Merrys came running to catch me up, 'You were wonderful in the masque, Mattie.'

I smiled coolly and asked her if she could run and get my shawl. She hesitated a moment and I stared her out, we stood frozen for a moment. Power had shifted and hung in the balance, then she nodded and ran off to fetch it.

My father is right. I do catch on quickly. I can help Katherine and my family and hold my own with those silly girls. I'm beginning to see the way councils, governments and advisors work. Maybe I could help some of the King's physicians with some new ideas. I could influence the future of English history. Very soon we may have a Howard as Queen, with a clever, peace-loving advisor who could improve things for poor people.

The Cobweb Mirror

I haven't been able to write in you, journal, for two days, we've been so busy preparing for Lent.

Lent at court doesn't seem nearly as bad as Katherine said. At home we were only allowed to eat boiled fish...and pears of course. But here, although we don't eat meat, we do have chicken. The King has ruled that chicken doesn't count as meat. It's a sort of fish apparently.

So we still have every type of poultry. Pheasants, baked inside turkeys, baked inside swans. And stargazy pies with little fish-heads staring out of the top. And blackbirds baked in coffins.

Although there are no masques of course, or dancing, or music. Except for holy psalms sung after dinner, which are really boring.

At dinner tonight, Nat Wootton, who Merry now says she is in love with - he's a show-off and very vain - reached noisily for some more wine, just as the King was nearing the end of a funny story. The King shouted and actually hit Nat round the head - as though he was boxing a little boy's ears. Half in jest, but, actually, not really. We all froze. Nat mumbled profuse apologies and bowed and left the table. Backwards as we have to, but a bit fast so he stumbled. He was so humiliated and the King roared with laughter at him.

Merry was terrified. Then Thomas Cromwell made a pleasantry and Katherine begged the King to tell us what happened at the end of the story and the atmosphere was restored. Merry looked very pale and ate no more syllabub.

I think the lack of meat makes the King crosser. But, as Katherine says, it will soon be Easter and then we'll have picnics and hunting and parties on the river and outdoor masques. And then the great May Day joust itself.

At midnight we tried, 'husband gazing.' We looked out at the full moon, holding the cobweb hand-mirror over our shoulders. When you reflect the moon over your face it is said you see your future husband. Katherine giggled nervously.

'Do you see a crown?' I asked her, '…and broad shoulders and red hair and piles of jewels…' Katherine's eyes shone in the moonlight.

I saw only the waxing moon and my own pale face.

The Easter Princess

It is Easter and little princess Elizabeth – the King's daughter by Anne Boleyn, is come to visit at Hampton Court. Katherine and I both adore her.

I play with her under the horse chestnut trees. It's warm for spring. She runs about, gathering up big armfuls of daisies for me.

She is so clever at her books – I think she reads and writes better than Katherine and she is only six. She's learning Latin and Greek and French.

She asked me so many questions as we lay knotting buttercups into wreaths, looking up at the clouds. Questions about the angels and the phases of the moon and alchemy and the four humours. It made me realise how much I miss my books. I only really have small snatches of thoughtful talk now, as I'm so rarely alone with Cecily.

Elizabeth wove buttercups in my hair, lifting off my hood. I looked like a maid of honour at a wedding already.

A page arrived to summon Elizabeth to the knot garden to join the King and her half-sister, Princess Mary – the King's daughter by his first wife Catherine. I watched the King throw her high in the air. She shrieked in ecstasy as her beloved bear-father caught her and swung her round and round.

I thought of my own dear, anxious father – he would never have tossed me carelessly into the air like that. I thought of how few years little Elizabeth had with her mother. What was it like to know that your adored father had ordered your mother's head to be chopped off with a sword? What would become of the little princess?

Thomas Cromwell came to call the King away. His clever fox face looked very anxious. I think I can guess why. The King barked at Cromwell, suddenly furious. Elizabeth left reluctantly and came cantering back to me, her eager pale face lit up beneath her flame of hair.

Maybe the King would be a kind husband for Katherine. Queen Anne doesn't seem to love him either. And then Katherine could bring poor little Elizabeth to live with us.

Katherine had been watching them in the garden too. We saw Cromwell follow him down to the pier where the royal barge was waiting. Four men – Culpepper among them - around him. Hard to believe a fifteen year old girl would love the older man, rather than a gorgeous young one, with violet eyes.

Katherine flung herself down beside us and Elizabeth poured flowers into her lap. Merry came running over, gabbling, and we had to make her slow down. She loves to be the first with a piece of gossip.

'Meggy was listening outside the council chamber… apparently the Queen wasn't ever actually free to marry and was promised to some old German prince and she doesn't have some papers, or something, to say she could even get married…' She paused for breath, '…and now the King says they've never had a proper marriage at all…' I glanced at little Elizabeth but she seemed busy with her flowers.

Can the King really have made this happen because he so loves Katherine? She gripped my hand till it hurt.

A Ruby Throat

I am writing in another new bed. We're back in London, this time at Westminster Palace.

Uncle sent for me before we left, which got me out of some of the endless packing, but he still makes me quake. I think I am learning to play him at his own game, though. Learning to be a clever shadow.

He told me, 'It is not enough that he is besotted with her. You must see to it that he has time alone with her at Westminster. She must lead him on further. There are many other pretty girls at court.'

I told him about the sickly 'Rose without a thorn' thing again and he said, 'Make sure she remains that way.'

The King is always surrounded by his men and she is always in a gaggle of Ladies in the Queen's rooms, but I will do my best.

We were in the Queen's privy chamber after dinner, packing. Katherine stroked the sable furs which the King gave Queen Anne as a wedding present. Then she picked up the necklace of royal rubies and held them up to her neck in the mirror, which of course she shouldn't do.

As she twirled, firefly sparks darted about the walls. She was lit up with excitement. I wonder how many Queens' necks those rubies have encircled?

She stopped twirling and stood with the blood red jewels at her throat. I could see she was filled with a new determination.

Then the great household was on the move, for the long ride back to London.

A Shoe Ribbon

I'm trying to get used to another set of rooms and corridors and servants to trust.

But I did it! I arranged for Katherine to be alone with the King this afternoon. My Uncle could not do better. I am becoming as skilled as Thomas Cromwell.

We were in the corridor with all the Merrys, on our way to play cards with the Queen. The King was coming in from the river with his men – including Culpepper, who I was pleased to see Katherine turned away from, with a toss of her hair.

I whispered to her to stop and tie the ribbon on her shoe, 'But it's not undone, Mattie…' she said. Then she caught on and bent down, while the other girls and I hurried on. The King ordered his men to leave him.

They had a full four minutes together on a window seat. Katherine said he called her a rose again and even gave her a kiss, 'His breath was foul and I could smell something else horrid, but he hinted that he's sending me a really big present tomorrow. I told him he looked handsome after his day on the river and he seemed very pleased.'

I've noticed the smell too. Cecily told me what it is. It's an old jousting wound that becomes poisonous and swells up and oozes pus. It has to be drained several times a day. When you get near him you can smell it quite strongly. It must be very painful. The wound has to be kept open so it doesn't trap the poisons inside it.

I told her I'd get some rosemary to put in her pomander, for when she's near the King, to disguise the smell. I told her that when the wound was drained it mightn't be so bad and she wouldn't notice it. Then I took her mind off it and wondered what the present might be…

An Extremely Big Present

Today the present arrived. Well, news of the present. It is an extremely big present. He's given her two houses! We can hardly believe it. Before she came to court all she owned in the world was about four dresses and a couple of hoods. She is entranced with the idea of having so much power.

Meggy skipped in, puffed up with news. More rumours 'They say the Queen's marriage is definitely not legal and it might be going to be something called annunned.'

'Annulled,' I said.

'Yes, well…it means it's over and the King can choose someone else. Which he has to do, to get another son to be an heir to the throne' finished Meggy.

Cecily was standing quietly beside her. I guessed she was the one who had heard the news. She looked gravely at me and then at Katherine.

'But he's got Prince Edward…' said Katherine.

I explained that it was in case Prince Edward dies. Because then only Princess Mary or Elizabeth would be in line to the throne. Though I don't know what's wrong with a woman being on the throne. I think Little Elizabeth would make a wonderful Queen.

But if Katherine marries the King and has a son…

I dance a volta!

Our cousin Anne Boleyn

The King is huge!

Princess Elizabeth is so sweet

82

I miss Caspian ♡

K's new brooch ♡ from Thomas

Katherine's hair shines like silk

83

A Surprise

We are all excited about the May Day joust tomorrow. Though I have become quite used to parties and entertainments. I shall go to bed early tonight, after braiding Katherine's hair. She's going to wear it wavy and flowing tomorrow.

I had just got into bed when there was a rapping on the window. The Hawk has me sharing with sweaty Meggy again, now we're at Westminster. At least she knows she has to give me the best side now and most of the coverlet. I went to the window and found Lettyce.

She'd found her way to me with the help of her sister, Pob, who works in the laundry. She said she'd come, 'To show me a bit of life', like she'd promised. I was happy to see her, of course, but had to laugh. What more of life could I want to see than at the finest court in the world!

She had a bag of poor-person clothes for me. A fashionable court lady would be pick-pocketed or attacked. She made me put on a foul, brown dress over my night-shift, rough boots and a cap. She pulled me out of the window, through a warren of laundries and kitchens, full of toiling servants - I didn't even know those places existed. Out into a back courtyard and through palace gates, into the city itself.

It felt very different, being amongst the stink of the crowds, rather than riding above it on horseback. It was exciting. Nobody paid me any attention. I like that. I feel powerful and free in the shadows.

Lettyce herself looked filthy. Was she really, once, my only friend? A pot of piss swished out of a doorway, and she pulled us out of the way as it narrowly missed our skirts, and we both laughed. It was lovely to be able to run again.

Rank fleshy smells came from a street of butchers' shops. Flaming torches in the dusk lit up a bear, which was being baited by a circle of rough men with snarling dogs. The bear was scrawny and covered in sores. They urged it on, in a stink of ale and sweat.

We crossed an alley and ran right up against the great flame of a fire-eater's breath and grasped each others hands, giggling with excitement at the shock of it. He blew another great fiery cloud at us and people applauded.

Lettyce chattered away, 'So what's it like? Is your cousin kind? Is the King handsome?' As we got nearer the river, she stopped. 'I've got another surprise for you, Miss Matilda Look!'

She pointed through the twilight, as though she were conjuring up a wonder: waiting at the corner was a tall, scruffy boy with a shock of black hair. 'This is Percy, Miss.'

He had a lopsided, wry smile and dark blackcurranty eyes. Even though I'm used to hundreds of really sophisticated boys, I suddenly didn't know what to say. All the things I used to imagine about him. It made me blush.

Percy seemed to be almost laughing at me with his smiley eyes. I wished I was wearing my court dress. He has filthy fingernails and wears rough clothes. Well, he is only a gardener at the Tower of London, I reminded myself. So I don't know why he wasn't more on his best manners. I tossed my hair and curtseyed graciously, like Katherine does when she's showing a boy she's not interested in him. He bowed but I felt he was somehow making fun of me, and I flushed again. It was really annoying.

I asked Lettyce where we were going, 'You know how you used to want to meet our mother and all the children…' Lettyce said, as a sweet-seller thrust a tray of dirty-looking sugar mice at us. Lettyce looked longingly at them.

'You should see the marchpane animals we have at Court.' I said, 'Every creature you could imagine. Dozens at every dinner…I must send you some.'

'Percy gets to see real lions and monkeys at the royal menagerie in the Tower, don't you Percy?' Lettyce said.

'I do – and the men's chopped-off heads and tortured bodies that have been stretched on the racks…'

Lettyce squealed with delight.

'Yes, well the King must punish traitors,' I said.

I told them how generous and funny Katherine is and how she makes everything an adventure. About my masque dress and eating peacocks. I thought it would be exciting for them to hear about court life.

They exchanged a look when we reached the public pier and Percy winked at Lettyce. I think they were envious because I heard Lettyce whisper to Percy, 'Katherine this and Katherine that,' which was a bit of a cheek.

We got on a wherry boat and Percy paid the man a coin and we travelled down the river through the darkness. We were crammed in amongst rough men and dogs and exhausted women carrying bundles of rags. It was very different to the royal barge and piers lit up by torch-bearing servants, with drums banging for the oarsmen to slide the oars in and out of the treacly water.

The house was reached through a maze of narrow, dark alleys. I was glad I had the old boots on and wasn't trying to get along on my fine shoes and chopines. The house was unbelievably tiny, but the rushes on the floor were clean and there was a fire burning. Actually it even smelt a bit better than the passageways at court do when the pissing places haven't been cleaned. There was no glass in the tiny windows though and the candles were of spitting tallow, not wax.

Their mother beamed at me. She was an almost exact copy of Lettyce, but fatter. I smiled at all the brothers and sisters, trying to look pleased and gracious like Katherine does when she's listening to religious music that she hates. There was rough, grey bread and sweaty-looking cheese laid out, especially for me. I didn't dare accept any for fear of infection with The Sweat, or worse.

I was glad I wasn't wearing my court dress, as the children looked filthy, 'This isn't my usual dress of course,' I said. Their mother laughed, 'I know, Miss Matilda, it's one of mine. One of my best ones!'

The children chased about, laughing and clambering all over her, while she fed the baby with milk from her own, sore-looking, breast. For a moment it all seemed rather jolly and cosy and I wanted to join in the romp too. I started to chase the littlest one, but then I felt Percy watching me and I remembered myself.

Six of them share one of the beds and five the other. I started to feel quite faint with the noise and the squash of bodies. As soon as was polite I said that it had been delightful to meet them all, but I should return to the Palace or the Queen might be anxious for me.

Percy looked at me as though he was amused by something. Not respectfully at all but their mother smiled kindly and curtseyed politely.

I was even thankful to be back on the wherry. Lettyce and Percy both seemed disappointed in me in some way. As we passed under London Bridge, torchlight lit up a row of rotting heads, displayed on spikes. Traitors beheaded by the King. The people in the boat jeered at them and I shivered.

Percy leaned in and said, 'They were probably dancing and eating your sugar peacocks last week,' I tossed my head like Katherine does.

Lettyce took my hand in the darkness, 'You have to be careful of court people Miss Matilda. You can't trust them all. Remember what your mother said? You can't play their game easy. Those ones up there probably thought they were clever last week'

I straightened my back and said witheringly, 'When I need advice from a servant and a gardener's boy, I'll make sure and ask you. I am the close friend of someone who is soon to be the most powerful person in England.'

'You need a powerful kick up your backside Miss Matilda, that's what you need,' said Percy. I flushed hot with rage and, as soon as we reached the pier I strode away from them. He let out a great hoot of laughter. What an obnoxious boy! How dare he!

Arghghhh! It makes me want to scream. Just wait till Katherine is Queen.

I walked into the labyrinth of alleyways. I was seething with rage and Lettyce called after me. 'That i'n't the way to the Palace, Miss Matilda…Come back!' I walked on through a dark passageway and Lettyce followed. 'I've had enough of you and your impertinent oaf of a brother! Leave me alone,' I shouted.

The passageway narrowed to a dead end. There was a burst of laughter in the darkness behind me and suddenly, I felt a filthy hand clamp over my mouth. In a stink of drinky breath, two stout, ragged girls of about eighteen had grabbed me, and then Lettyce. They rummaged my pockets.

'Let's see what you got, lady-voice!' Their brown rotted teeth stank. A leg clamped my shins, hurting me. Lettyce screamed and fought furiously.

I bit my girl's hand and struggled but couldn't get away. She was so strong. A moment later she swore and dropped me: Percy had crept up silently and grabbed her arms from behind. From the ground, I managed a vicious kick at the other girl, who had Lettyce, and she was free. Lettyce spat in her face. The girls ran off into the night, swearing a torrent of oaths at us.

I somehow felt even more furious with Percy, as I picked myself up, scowling. He raised his eyebrows and smiled again, 'No need to thank me, Miss.' and strode off. Insufferable boy.

Lettyce grabbed my arm and we walked quickly towards the Palace. I was so shocked and cross, I couldn't find a word for her either. Lettyce delivered me angrily and silently to my window. By now I felt a bit foolish. I'd put us both in danger.

In my room I pulled the rough clothes off and gave them back to her. Thank goodness the Merrys were still up dancing. I didn't know what to say to Lettyce. Anyway I wouldn't have had that awful fright if she hadn't come tonight.

Neither of us spoke. Lettyce was very formal. She curtseyed instead of hugging me good-bye, which she didn't need to have done. But perhaps it is for the best. She gave me two letters from home. I thanked her and wrote a quick note to Frances and mother, though I suddenly felt at a loss as to what to say and my hands were shaking slightly.

'Well Miss, stay safe,' she said. As an afterthought I thrust my old hood into her hands. She didn't seem at all pleased, but took it and was quickly away out of the window.

I feel so far beyond her now. I may soon be Chief Lady-in-Waiting and adviser to the new Queen of England. I feel I've left Lettyce far behind on a distant shore.

Of course I'll always feel affection for her. Maybe I can find her a place as a servant of the bath one day.

I felt strange after she'd gone and now I find tears running down my face for no reason at all.

The Joust

I didn't sleep well and had taunting, restless dreams.
Katherine and I were entwined with ivy, which was growing
around us so that we could not get apart. Lettyce was trying
to free me from the ivy and I was pushing her away, whilst
wanting to be free. The ivy wound itself round my throat.

Meggy dug me in the ribs to stop me moaning and I kept
waking through cracks in the night, covered in a light sweat.

But this morning was exciting, getting ready for the May
Day joust and I put Lettyce quite out of my mind.

Katherine wore the new golden gown and she has given me
her rose silk one. We walked down the corridor arm in arm,
with our hair in long waves, dark and fair. All the Merrys and
Cecily stood back and watched us as though we were in a
pageant. It's so funny the way they all want to be like us, or
be with us, trying to make us laugh and giving us little gifts.

That is what court gives you if you are clever enough.
Like Thomas Cromwell and Uncle and Katherine and me.
To think that only a few months ago they were laughing
at my stockings.

I must do something kind to help Cecily. I will make the Merrys be nice to her. And have a lovely basket of sweetmeats sent to Lettyce's mother. If you have power you must use it well.

I had a sudden thought and asked Cecily to come back into our room. Katherine has given me two of her gowns. I could transform Cecily for the joust.

I took off her awful old gown and hood and put on one of my French ones from Katherine, pushing it back on her head so that it was much more flattering and plaited her hair at the back and gave her one of my lawn shifts to wear under Frances' russet velvet dress. It was at least a better colour than hers.

She flushed when she saw herself in the mirror and thanked me quietly, but she didn't seem very pleased. Almost as though she were afraid of me – she reminded me of one of the Queen's lap dogs. I felt the little prickly feeling again and we nodded awkwardly and said we'd see each other at the joust. I was rather irritated.

The joust was a blur of colour, dust, thundering hooves, trumpeting, puffed-up chivalry and pulsing drum beats thudding though my chest. It's like the legends of King Arthur I used to read. The King loves King Arthur.

The Queen sat up high in the royal box and had to drop a handkerchief at the start of each fight. Then the two, 'knights' on dressed-up horses, came running at each other with long poles and tried to knock each other off.

I didn't find it as exciting as everyone else did. I was worried the horses might get poked in the eye, which made me think of Caspian, which made me think of Lettyce and gave me the odd prickling feeling again.

But Katherine adored it and she had favourites she urged on. Thomas Culpepper is the best rider. The King cheered him on too.

I could see Katherine was studying how the Queen dropped the handkerchief and garlanded the winners with basil leaves 'I'd love to have them all fighting over me, like Queen Gwenigwoo, or whatever her name was,' she whispered to me.

Queen Anne looks serious. How must she feel, knowing people are saying she isn't properly married to the King. He might have her executed, like cousin Anne. Or accuse her of being a witch and have her burnt. Or lock her in the Tower for ever. I feel sorry for her. I was a bit cross to see that Cecily had pulled the hood right back down over her hair. Honestly, some people just don't want to be helped!

The King's gaze kept wandering to Katherine in her glimmering gown. Uncle gave me a grim, approving nod from the shadows. He must be pleased with me. I think it is beginning.

I wonder where we shall be this time next May Day?

Confusion

We have been thrown into a spin. The King is sending the Queen away to Richmond Palace. He says he's worried about her catching the plague in London. Most of the Pumpkin Heads are going with her. But Katherine is being sent back to her grandmother's house in Lambeth and I, and a couple of the Merrys, are to go with her. We don't know what to think: Is it good? Is it bad? Is it terrible?

We're so scared she has done something wrong. Maybe she shouldn't have been flirting so openly with the King. Or he isn't pleased with her any more.

I sent a note to Uncle and we waited anxiously. He sent back to say that all is going perfectly to plan and we breathed again. He said Katherine is to continue just as she's doing.

She will receive 'secret visits' at Lambeth.

Katherine went white with excitement and gripped my hand, digging her nails into my wrist. 'Is it happening, Matilda?'

We packed hurriedly and took a royal barge across the river to Lambeth. The Merrys and The Hawk and I now seem to be sort of Ladies-in-Waiting to Katherine. But I know, of course, that I am actually her best friend and closest advisor.

Uncle sent me another note about, 'Spotless virtue and angelic behaviour,' and how 'sweet and ready,' she must be. What does he think she's been doing all this time!

Katherine has her own room and doesn't have to go back into the long-rooms where the Merrys and I sleep with dozens of other girls. I hate the long-rooms. The girls are so stupid and just talk about boys half the night. But they know they have to be very polite to me. Katherine is a bit sorry she can't take part in the midnight feasts any more, but she knows (and everyone knows) that she's about to be prepared for the biggest role of her life…royal bride to be.

It Is Happening

This morning swarms of dressmakers arrived. Katherine stood on a stool to be pinned into clouds of silk and taffeta. They rolled out bolt after bolt of azure and lilac and scarlet. A rainbow of stockings and ribbons and dancing-slippers and perfumed gloves. I began to rather tire of it all.

Katherine loves it of course. She has already become a bit Queenly in her manner and is sometimes quite bossy. She keeps telling me how important it is to get everything right and 'of the very latest French fashion.' So what!

In the evenings the King comes. He's sometimes slightly disguised. Like anyone could possibly not know who the huge old giant in a purple velvet doublet, sitting in the royal barge, is.

He has special dinners at a table with Katherine, though we have to be in the room. She smiles as though she's enchanted by him and in awe of his magnificence. Sometimes she acts like a nine year old and sometimes she acts like a thirty year old. The King gazes at her and seems really pleased with her, like she's something he's bought.

He eats a great deal, with puffy fingers like uncooked pastry. She's always grumpy and strained afterwards. But she loves the presents which arrive the next morning.

The dowager Agnes, Katherine's grandmother, has just called us to her. A settlement has been made on Queen Anne and the marriage is over. She's going to be known from now on as the 'King's sister'. We left the room all sober and dignified and then Katherine hugged me and we jumped up and down squealing. She was really gloating. 'Queen Anne will have to give all the royal jewels back...even the ruby necklace. Matilda, I'll get the ruby necklace!'

So, now everyone is in a tremendous flutter. The King is coming to supper tonight. We all think, well we know, that he is going to ask Lady Agnes and Uncle for her hand in marriage. As though he needed to! Ha!

Katherine says it doesn't feel real and that her head feels full of spun sugar. The King of England is coming to ask for her hand. It's like a fairytale. It's like a scene from a masque. Yes, in fact it is a scene that I have directed...

Later

It has happened. It is done. Now she has only two weeks to get a wedding gown made.

Secret Wedding

Well…The marriage has just taken place in secret. Katherine is rather put out about it. Hardly anyone was allowed to be there and there was only a very simple wedding breakfast afterwards.

The really shocking thing is something else. The King has had Thomas Cromwell executed. On the very day of the wedding. His closest advisor. All because Cromwell organised his wedding to Anne. It gives me a horrid, sick feeling. If he couldn't keep safe with all his cleverness and his staying in the shadows…

Katherine doesn't get a triumphal progress into London yet, which is making her really cross. But the King does seem to be truly in love. He kisses her and pets her all the time. Even in public. We're hearing a lot of the 'Rose without a thorn,' which makes me want to puke. They're having the honeymoon here but she says he's promised her proper parties later.

Tonight she has to sleep with the King for the first time in the Queen's privy chamber. Her privy chamber now. I cannot get used to it. No more pillow fights. We got her ready in a beautiful nightgown and plaited her hair elaborately. She looked terrified and had an odd smile frozen onto her face.

The King was brought in, supported by four of his men, who staggered under his bulk. Thomas Culpepper was among them, of course. Katherine was very careful not to look at him. The King's face was damp and swollen and his breath heavy. We all knelt and said prayers. I was trying to keep my eyes averted from the King, but I was grimly fascinated by his huge, bloated body in the night-shift as his dressing gown came off.

Now I am not blinded by all the magnificence around him, I can see he is just a terrifying, fat old man. His freshly-dressed wound smelled already. I feel so sorry for Katherine tonight. She will need my help more than ever now.

Being Queen

This morning Katherine was really cross and shouted at me when I brushed a tangle from her hair, 'He farts and sweats all night. He smells like rotten offal and boiled cabbage,' she said. It must be dreadful and I don't really know what to say. I tried to cheer her up by reminding her how much Meggy farts, but she became even more bossy and sort of cold. I am not surprised, after a night in that terrible bed.

I know she misses our knot of girls in the rooms – the gossiping and little dramas she ruled over. It feels very strange for me too, to have her as the real Queen and have to curtsey to her.

I thought Uncle might be pleased, but he's going on more than ever about how I must stop Katherine from flirting or even looking at another man. His yellow fingers knot like curdled milk, as he gives me his warnings.

The King's wound seems better today. It affects the daily mood of the whole court, depending on how raw it is and whether it's giving him fevers and headaches. That and the state of his bowels. He gets blocked up. Everyone knows about the state of both the wound and the bowels.

I would be interested to see the wound and how the surgeons dress it to keep the skin from sealing over so that they can drain the poison. I wonder if I could ask Thomas Culpepper.

I feel an odd, uncomfortable sensation when I think of Thomas. If I hadn't encouraged Katherine with the King, would they be happily engaged by now?

The Most Famous Girl In The World

Katherine was jittery with excitement as we set off for
Hampton Court. She had been practising gracious waves
to the crowd for hours. It was her first appearance in public
as Queen. She has her own royal barge. The King wrote a
motto for her which is painted on the side. It's in French, so
I translated it for her, 'Non autre volonte que la sienne': 'No
other will than his'. Which made her snort with laughter
when I told her. But then she saw the crowds and dug her
fingers into my wrist again.

Hampton Court has been done up especially for her. I feel
as though Katherine and I are at the top of a turret looking
down on all the court as the Merrys and the new girls vie for
our attention.

Of course she loves all her wonderful new things, but
Katherine is often withdrawn. When she is away from the
King and we're alone in her rooms, she becomes herself
again, romping around with her new dog Ribbons. Then
she's my giddy friend Katherine, again. For a while.

This afternoon when we were in her bedchamber, more
presents from the King were delivered: a huge diamond collar
and sables. Then she opened a casket and her face lit scarlet.
The royal rubies had arrived. As she tried the necklace on, her
eyes glinted triumphantly. It has circled Jane Seymour's neck,
Anne of Cleves' neck and now Katherine's.

I couldn't help wondering if the dead wives ever come back to haunt the living ones. Would their ghosts envy the new queens, or want to warn them?

She threw the presents onto the bed in gloating piles, on top of that day's newly-finished dresses. Forty new ones had been ordered before the wedding. She flung herself on top of the rainbow heap, burying herself in the silk and furs, 'Do you think I am the richest and most famous fifteen year old in the world?' She asked.

She stretched her arms languidly then started to dance round the room in her shift, laden with the rubies till blood-red sparks flashed urgently round the walls again. Then she wound pearls round my neck and grabbed me and we skipped about in a wild volta, laughing till I thought I might wet myself.

A page arrived with a message from the King. The wild moment was broken. She froze, then called for the Ladies to help her dress.

Looking in the mirror, she readied herself for more play-acting. She has to pretend that her husband is a gorgeous boy and not a bad-tempered, stinking old man. But he clearly adores her. Tonight she's going to give him the peppermint wash I made, so his breath won't smell so foul.

August

So hot. We are packing up, yet again, to begin a Progress, staying at castles all over the country. It will be good to leave the stinking palace.

There'll be lots of hunting, which I'm excited about. Katherine has wonderful new horses, of course, and is saving a fast, spirited one for me. There will be picnics and jousts and a big Masque in fresh country air. Maybe I will have time to get to my books again. I'm going to ask Cecily if she can get me some books. I'd like a medical one. It is good to see Cecily again after Lambeth, but she seems very nervous of me.

The journey is slow but Katherine adores being at the head of the great procession and I love my horse Bess. Outside the city gates a monastery was being knocked down. It seems so cruel for the monks and the poor villagers, here, who rely on them for charity and medicine. All the golden things go into the treasury to buy clothes and jewels and feasts, which would feed a village for a year.

A Golden Heart

We have stopped at a grand hunting lodge in a forest. The spending, even here, is starting to give me a sickly feeling. Katherine seems to think she needs a new dress every day. She gives lots to me of course. I have so many now.

This afternoon Katherine had a headache so I bathed her temples with rosewater and dabbed her all over with vinegar and camomile. I left her to rest and called Cecily into the best Ladies' room, where I sleep.

Cecily seemed anxious that she might be in trouble. She curtseys to me now, which isn't necessary but The Hawk has told her this is court etiquette. Katherine thinks it's hilarious. I don't want Cecily to feel like that with me and fear me. I blushed to see she prefers to wear her old clothes and hood, rather than the ones I gave her. I know I was showing off when I did that.

I asked her to sit on the bed next to me. She told me she knows how to slip into the book rooms in every palace and can fetch books for me, without anyone noticing, and that there are lots about medicine. She likes books about codes. She says they're useful and gave me a long serious look. She slipped a book under my pillow later. I fell asleep after reading late into the night about the circulation of the blood.

I dreamt that Katherine and I were tangled in each others hair. We couldn't get free no matter how we pulled, until it felt as though the roots would tear our scalps. I got up and leant out of the window and let the cool moonlight bathe my sticky face.

This morning when I saw my pinched face in the mirror, my ears studded with Katherine's emeralds, my jewelled hood, I had this odd feeling. As though I'd lost some bit of myself. I've stepped right through the mirror and can't get back. The other Matilda is left somewhere, maybe still in a pear tree in Norfolk, longing for a life of adventure. What did I use to imagine life at court was like? Surely not this darkly glittering place?

Uncle asks for frequent reports now of course, and I am able to say Katherine is performing her duties perfectly and tell him what the King says to her. I don't tell him that she is sometimes very low in spirits.

But she loves the hunting and we get up at dawn to ride and have picnics on the river. And then we watch the boys joust and sing for us.

Katherine comes truly alive at the night dances. Last night we all wore masks. Katherine was dancing opposite Thomas Culpepper for a long time. The King, who is too fat to dance himself now, seems to love watching her dance with his Favourite.

She made sure she smiled at her husband as though she was performing for his delight, of course. And she ran over to tell him, 'You are the most handsome man here by far.' And he believed her.

After the dance she looked unusually happy. She wrapped her arm round my waist like she used to. But I soon found out why. She slipped a little note into my sleeve. It was to take it to Thomas Culpepper. Tonight my mask didn't make me feel safe. I knew how dangerous this was. Terribly dangerous. But Katherine looked so happy. I walked calmly over and entered the maze of the dance.

When Thomas came near and we joined hands to form an arch, I slipped the note into his palm. For an instant, I thought I caught sight of Uncle's face in a mirror watching us, and my heart skipped a beat. But when I turned to look, he seemed not to have seen anything. When Thomas came dancing down the room again he smiled and passed me something in a little velvet bag. A simple, golden heart brooch pierced with an arrow.

I shudder now to think what would happen if my Uncle suspected. Uncle. Or the King. I'm not so sure I still want to be the keeper of secrets…but I want Katherine to be happy again. It is so horrible for her sometimes with that fat old man. I know that I got her into this, and that I must help her to make it bearable…

Return

The King is exhausted. Well, a fifty year old man, trying to keep up with a fifteen year old wife, would be! We are back at Hampton Court and he is closed in his rooms with a fever. His wound is inflamed and infected. He is in a vile mood and this morning thundered at Nat Wootton for dropping a jug and swore him out of his sight.

His bowels are blocked up too. He sits on his special black velvet, gold-studded 'jakes' with a 'Valet of the Stool' to help him, for hours. But he still eats the rich foods that make him even fatter and more ill.

Not that Katherine is too worried about his diet. She doesn't really care about anything that isn't Thomas Culpepper. It's not just that he's handsome and a good dancer and makes her laugh...I think it may be the first strong, true feeling she's ever had for anyone – apart from our friendship.

This morning I helped her write a note to Thomas. Her writing is so bad. I tried to put my Uncle's orders out of my head, because I want her to be happy like this. If she's happy it'll be easier for her to keep the King happy. As long as no one ever finds out it will be alright. And I will be careful that no one does.

Autumn

The nights draw in and the mornings are frosty when I walk out with the dogs. This is when I have time to think about the books Cecily brings me.

The parties have stopped while the King is ill. It is a relief not to see all the wasted food and the dressmakers simpering in every day to make new frocks. Katherine can think only of Thomas now and their secret meetings. She calls him Tom.

I love the astronomical clock. It shows the sun revolving round the earth and the phases of the moon. I love the way the moon waxes and wanes throughout a month. Especially now I have started to bleed. So when I feel sad and cramping, I think about the moon and it seems to come into my dreams to guide me.

Christmas

Christmas time is here – with masques and endless feasts of roasted meats and heavy puddings and spiced wines. The King is feeling better and the gifts have started to pour again. The extravagance of the King's presents to his 'little rose, Kitty' is dizzying.

This afternoon she was lying on her bed cuddling Ribbons and listlessly stacking gifts onto the counterpane, 'There are thirty-three diamonds in this brooch and sixty six rubies… so he must love me,' she said. She likes counting them. It seems to reassure her, though she doesn't count very easily or want me to teach her how to do it properly.

She tried on a muffler of velvet strewn with pearls, wrapped it round Ribbons and then tossed it on the floor, bored. Ribbons started to chew it.

Even Queen Anne, I mean the last Queen – now the 'King's sister' - gave her a Christmas gift. A horse dressed in purple velvet. Katherine is generous to little Princess Elizabeth, though, and gives her lots of little trinkets and lets her sit near her at the feasts. We both love her. She comes out with such wicked funny remarks at odd moments. At seven, she is already wiser than Katherine.

Katherine hadn't thought about a gift for Lady Anne and gave her an old ring and a couple of her uglier lapdogs that she didn't like much, saying, 'It must be so odd for you that I used to be your Maid and now I'm wearing the royal rubies.' But I don't think Lady Anne is sad about it at all.

Katherine gives me so many dresses but I'd really rather have the books Cecily fetches for me. I can't help thinking that one pearl from her muffler could feed Lettyce's family for the rest of their lives and that her tiny sisters wouldn't have to work swilling floors and scrubbing linen.

New Year's Eve

The New Year's Eve banquet was merry and I enjoyed seeing Katherine look so happy and beautiful. As the toasting cup went round I felt suddenly an outsider looking in again. I have come a long way from the excited little girl catching the Queen's piss under the table.

Lettyce appeared this morning to say thank you for the Christmas gifts. At least I could send fine things for her family and mine. I felt so aware of how grand my room and my brocade dress must look to her. I tried to hug her, but she was like a stiff doll in my arms.

I wanted to say I was sorry – though I wasn't exactly sure what for – and I wanted to ask after Percy, but somehow I couldn't. It was awkward really. She could see I was distressed and she warmed a little and asked my advice about the baby's croup and we talked a bit more easily.

As she turned to leave she whispered, 'Miss Matilda, if you ever need help, just get a message to me or Percy at our mother's.' I couldn't imagine, though, how she thought she could ever help me. Here. This was another world entirely.

Cecily came into the room with a book for me and I introduced them. Cecily put Lettyce at her ease straight away and I was a little annoyed. It was another rather awkward parting and afterwards I thought of all the funny, easy things I should have tried to say.

I hid under the coverlet for a while and held my charm necklace and thought about Mother and my new baby brother and Caspian and Hunter and home.

It is painfully chill now the twelve days of Christmas are over. Winter settles in the bone and frost flowers creep over the window panes. My heart feels frozen too. But not Katherine's. All her thoughts turn on Thomas now.

She even has less time for her clothes. I can do nothing but help her to meet him as safely as possible and to conceal it from Uncle. And from the King.

Another Birthday

It was a very quiet birthday today. I feel a wiser fourteen year old. Can it really be a year since I set out from home so full of excitement?

Katherine is not what I thought her to be. She is enchanting and you put on her whatever you want to see. The King sees one girl, I see another and Thomas another. She is like some kind of mirror in a story that reflects back what you want to see in it.

Shrove Tide

The King is ill after all the feasting at Christmas. His face has gone black as his leg ulcer is infected again, and his doctors work day and night to release the poison from it. I peeped into the anteroom of surgeons preparing their instruments. They were examining bowls of blood and pus and his stools.

Katherine isn't allowed in to see him and is frightened that he is tiring of her, which would be dangerous, but she's so relieved not to have to be near him, especially when his festering wound stinks more than ever. I must make her take care.

The usual celebrations before Lent aren't happening at all this year. There will be no big Masque. I think of last year, when I pushed Katherine towards the fireworks and into the limelight. I don't mind Lent coming. I will be quite happy to eat less and think more.

Katherine is moaning about Lent already, 'I won't be able to wear my rubies, or dance with Tom or listen to my music.'

While the King is ill Katherine has been able to see more of Thomas. The King likes to have Thomas by him, day and night, often sleeping in his chamber. But he comes to give us frequent reports on how the King slept or whether his bowels have opened.

A Warning

This morning I was asking Thomas about the King's treatments. He told us, 'To keep the wound from healing over full of poisons, they put gold pieces in it and thread twine through it to pull it apart. So he will have to live with a permanently open wound from now on.'

Katherine got fed up, 'Ugh. Can't you two stop talking about all this blood and pus? It's so boring and depressing.'

I left them alone while I kept watch outside the door. It had only been a few minutes when I saw one of Uncle's men, coming towards me down the corridor. I started to sing loudly, which was the warning signal, to alert Katherine and Thomas inside. My heart was thundering, but he bowed and passed by.

My Heart Skips A Beat

Today Katherine is frantic because Thomas is ill with a fever. Of course she can't go and see him, but sent me with one of my remedies.

Later I helped her write him a long letter. She can still barely write – though I try to teach her. Strange how Lettyce learnt in a flash. Katherine took so long to form the letters, but she does feel what she writes.

Katherine asked me to take a velvet cap and jewelled brooch with the letter. I wrapped them in silk, to hide in my sleeve, but it was a bulky package and the letter was sticking out. I pulled my veil over my hood. I was nearing the antechamber to the King's rooms, where the Grooms-of-the-Chamber sleep, when Cecily came hurrying towards me. Her eyes flashed a warning and I tugged down my sleeve.

She is good at hiding in shadows too. To my astonishment, she pulled the bundle out of my sleeve and turned her back to the wall by a window seat.

Uncle walked out of the room I had just been about to enter. 'What have you there, child?' he barked. Cecily had somehow managed to conceal the letter and cap and all I was left with was the piece of silk. I curtseyed and showed him.

My thoughts raced but I managed a fairly calm, 'Good evening to you, Uncle,' and told him it was a sample of cloth that Katherine planned to embroider as a handkerchief for the King and that she'd sent me to match it to his new doublet.

His eyes narrowed suspiciously in his tallow face. The story was ridiculous. The thought of Katherine sewing! But he nodded and said, 'I see. A sweet, wifely thought.' My heart was pushing against my ribs and I felt faint as he walked away. Cecily pulled the letter and cap from underneath her bum-roll and walked off too, without a word.

Henricus Rex

Katherine called for me in the night. She couldn't sleep.
I gave her some valerian and sat on her bed. 'Henry hasn't
sent me a single trinket for so long, and look…what does
this mean, on the end of this note?' she asked. It was signed
Henricus Rex, instead of the heart he usually draws, 'It just
means King Henry,' I told her, 'Oh. In French?' she said.
I told her it was Latin and she tossed her head impatiently.

'Oh well yes, foreign, same thing. Why is everything so
boring and serious all of a sudden?' she wailed, and told me
that Uncle had come to see her this afternoon and asked
her, 'quite horridly', why she wasn't pregnant yet because
she has to get 'an heir for England.' He also asked her how
her embroidery was progressing, which totally confused her.
'Why's he going on about embroidery now? I just want to
have fun again, and be with Thomas. It's not fair.' Her big
eyes filled with tears.

'Thomas will be better soon,' I told her, 'And so will the King
and there's plenty of time to have a baby. You're only sixteen.'

I stroked her hair till she slept. I give her concoctions
of mare's milk, sheep's urine and rabbit's blood every
morning, to help her get pregnant. They taste vile and often
make her puke.

Our cousin Anne managed to give the King a healthy daughter. Little Elizabeth. But she was killed for not having a son. The King is so old and sick and must be fearing he'll die leaving only one male heir. If Prince Edward does die then Katherine's son would be King…

I think Katherine hopes, secretly, that the King will die and she will marry Thomas. But she also fears and respects the King so much she muddles him up with God. Well, he does say he's head of the Church. I think sometimes she feels he can see everything she's doing

The physician side of me feels sorry for the King being in so much pain, but I also see he is a mad bully and that he's becoming madder. He has so many terrifying outbursts now, for no reason.

Since he had Thomas Cromwell killed, I have started to notice how many people disappear to the Tower.

Cecily and I heard whisperings about all the Catholic monks and nuns he's having burnt and tortured and imprisoned. She told me about the terrible torture devices in the Tower. One is called The Skeffington's Daughter, which is a small iron cage you have to crouch in. It's clamped to your legs and arms and they make it smaller and smaller and leave you in it in the dark for days.

Everyone is fawning over the King more and more, for fear his temper might suddenly snap, and they'll be next.

A Dance

The King is feeling better, and was up this evening, watching
Katherine dance for him, with Thomas. It is so ironic. He
said Thomas reminds him of his young self and behaves
as though they are three young friends together. Katherine
is giddy with joy tonight. I stood by the window and she
came to lean her hot head on my shoulder, 'Oh Mattie, I'm
so happy.' Outside, a sky of midnight blue scattered with
diamonds, like a blown dandelion clock. Across the room
I saw Uncle watching us with suspicion.

'Please, please be careful, Katherine,' I whispered. She sighed
and skipped over to sit on the King's lap.

Soon we leave on the summer Progress – I must convince
her to be more careful…there are so many eyes and ears at
court, listening at every door. I thought I could play this
game – I was so naïve. I don't sleep well at night, myself.

Summer Progress

Katherine couldn't decide what to take and about a hundred gowns had to be packed in lavender. Endless ropes of jewels were stuffed into chests. And Ribbons along with the other lap dogs put into baskets and nightingales into cages. I felt listless but had to summon up energy to control the whirl.

In the midst of the packing, Katherine decided to have a pillow fight and scattered half the things we'd folded, onto the floor. Ribbons jumped around in them. I feel like her mother sometimes. I just long for – I don't know – something: the sense of wonder when you look at the stars or the astronomical clock or the waxing moon. And I do feel a creeping fear.

Cecily says the King had the Countess of Salisbury executed today. The executioner had to hack at her head several times as she crawled away from the block. Uncle asked me again if Katherine thinks of anyone else. I lied.

At last we were packed up and the cavalcade left. I long for fresh country air and the hunting and to be able to gallop Bess, wild and free.

I miss Caspian 💟

Too Many Secrets

Katherine loves the Progress. There are masques and picnics at every new place. She made us all dress in Lincoln green today (to enter into Lincoln), with the King as Robin Hood (as huge as a house) and Katherine as Maid Marion. Merry and Nat Wootton looked like a couple of string beans.

When we reach York there's going to be a joust to celebrate Henry meeting King James. Katherine is already practising how to preside over the joust. She's thinking of little else but Thomas winning her favours and how she's going to crown him with basil leaves.

The King, more than ever, seems to want to see Thomas as his young self, jousting in his place.

Thomas rode up alongside us this morning and slipped a note into my hand. I hid it quickly in my riding glove. He is not careful enough, either. They seem to think themselves so safe just because the King loves them both. It is madness. My Uncle's words ring in my ears. I am tired of secrets.

Lincoln Castle is an old place, full of secret passageways. I have just got back to my bed and cannot stop shaking. This evening they were reckless again. Thomas ran up the spiral stairs to meet Katherine in her turret room, before I had given the signal that all the ladies were in bed. As I stood on guard at the foot of the stairs, The Hawk appeared.

'Matilda, what was Thomas Culpepper doing on the back stair to the Queen's room?' she hissed. I told her he was bringing us news of the King's bad stomach and that I had given him a rubbing tincture to collect for the King. Will she tell Uncle? I will tell Katherine to give her a present tomorrow.

Narrow Escape

At least here at Hull we are staying in tented pavilions outside and surely there is no way Katherine can secretly meet Thomas. She hunts with him and the King. Today the King slaughtered 200 deer and swans. It is like a charnel house. But it makes him feel young and vigorous to kill things.

Today we were picnicking in a beautiful orchard. I bit into a pear and felt a rush of shame. I have lost myself. I have quite lost my pear-tree self in this glittery, false world.

Cecily glanced over at me and smiled. I flushed again remembering how I patronised her, dressing her in my cast-offs. What a good friend she is to me, with our book expeditions and quiet talks. Katherine saw me smile back and tugged me up, clapping for music, 'Come on Mattie, stop being boring. Let's show the boys some dancing,' she shouted. She smelled of candied quinces and rosewater as she began to dance.

All eyes were on her, in her shimmery gown and that is what she loves. She wants to live in a masque. You just want to gaze at her and imagine things, but there is so little really there. Does she know that herself, I wonder?

My heart is knocking in my chest. When the King was snoring heavily, Katherine appeared in my masque disguise and pulled me into her pavilion. She pushed me into her bed and put her lacy nightcap over my head, 'Matilda you're queen for a night…don't worry the King won't visit you…if he does you'll just have to put up with it!' She laughed hysterically at the sight of my face, 'Keep your head under the covers in case The Hawk comes in. She sleeps soundly though. She's had so much wine. I am you. How lucky you are to be free.' And she slipped off to meet Thomas by the lake.

I lay under the royal silk sheets with my heart pounding and my thoughts racing. I heard footsteps outside. If it was The Hawk she would surely recognise my shape and go straight to Uncle.

Time stood still. The footsteps came closer and then moved away again. It was the night guard. I must never let her be so reckless again. I must have slept at last for I felt the bed shift. Oh God was it the King? But Katherine laughed and nestled in next to me, 'You are my truest friend and only solace Matilda. Don't be cross with us. Love is all and I love him so.'

'You could get us all killed,' I hissed. 'Oh Henry loves us, he would never want us to be sad.'

Pontefract

We have arrived at Pontefract Castle and Katherine has
already had me hunting out hidden passageways and
staircases. I look for the shadows.

A New Danger

Something bad has happened. Katherine's first love – Francis Dereham, the boy she met in the long rooms, has turned up. Here! The only way he says he will keep quiet is if she gives him a job as her private secretary. It is blackmail. And she has given him the job. It is madness.

If people find out that she had a boyfriend before the King – or if she's tempted to flirt with him again or even if he lets slip he used to know her …The King would find out. He will explode…How furious would he be? Would their marriage become invalid? What would he do to her? I must make her keep him silent. And keep them apart. And I am sure Francis is still in love with her.

I am caught in a web. If only there were someone I could talk to. Journal, you are my only friend. I daren't talk openly to Cecily, though I'm sure she knows everything. I'd draw her into the web too.

Katherine is so much in love she grows ever more careless. Anyone can see she's flirting with Thomas. More than flirting. That her eyes light up when he's near her. That she's in love. She takes so many risks. I know she just wants to be an ordinary sixteen year old girl. But she isn't ordinary.

She wanted the rubies and the dresses and now she has to behave like a Queen. Or else we'll both end up in The Tower. In the Skeffington's Daughter. Or on the block.

Sick

This morning Katherine swapped gifts with Thomas. She gave him a bracelet and he gave her a ring, which I have to wear for her, on the chain around my neck, with the key to the secret compartment. So I feel danger hanging at my throat all day long. Francis seems to watch her all the time, what if he discovers she is in love with Thomas? I am starting to feel sick a lot of the time.

Katherine and Thomas both think that because the King adores them, they are safe. It only means that to the King, their love would be unthinkable, unbearable.

The King and Uncle have spies everywhere. Am I clever enough to protect her?

King's Manor

We travel through the cool of the day and have at last reached King's Manor to wait for the great meeting between the two Kings. But King James does not come. We do not know why. But it is clearly not a good thing. Katherine was longing to be Queen of the joust, and is sulky. The King's mood is blackening.

Last Days of Summer

Part of me would love to run home to Norfolk, now we have started to make our way back south to Hampton Court. But how can I leave Katherine unprotected when it is my fault she is Queen? It is all my fault.

Our masque hairstyle

Poor Pumpkin Head Anne

Melly Buxton is a snake

Uncle will not help us now.

We enter the Tower by the Water Gate

We shall never leave

Windsor

The King's black despair is frightening her.

We have got as far as Windsor and there is more bad news.
Prince Edward has quartan fever. He's swollen and hot.
The King's longing for another son is even more urgent.
Katherine keeps asking me to make her new potions to help
her become pregnant, besides the ones the King's doctors
make for her.

The potions are very bitter and make her throw up but she
always says, 'Oh well, at least the puking keeps me slender.'
Such a stupid thing to say when Miggy made herself so ill
trying to be thin.

This morning, when we were playing cards, we heard that
little Prince Edward is better and her fear has lifted. The
King is calmer and we are on the move.

Hampton Court

Back at Hampton Court at last. The King seems fonder of 'little Kitty' than ever. He's had a fat new brooch made for her. 'Thirty five diamonds and eighteen rubies, Mattie,' she tells me as she tosses it into the casket with the others. She runs the jewels through her fingers like sweets. They make her feel safe.

'I'll have the goldsmith do earrings to match, like Autumn leaves. Tom loves my ears.' She rains kisses down on Ribbons' nose.

But I feel heavy. I watch reflections shivering on the black river and the garden full of fleeting shadows. The gardeners burning piles of leaves make me think of other burnings.

It is All Saints Day. The morning is wreathed with clammy fog from the river. The King has ordered that, in every church in England, people must say a special prayer of thanks for Katherine, 'His jewel of womanhood'. She says it's hilarious, but is delighted of course, 'It must be a good sign Mattie, mustn't it? And the brooch…but he's always around and I haven't seen Tom for days, I can't bear it.'

Francis Dereham comes in and out while we talk by the fire. It is so dangerous that he is her secretary. He's always asking if he can write a letter for her. As if Katherine wanted to send letters to anyone other than Thomas. Am I imagining it, or is Francis watching her with a new, threatening, jealous look?

If the King finds out about their past…She keeps swearing him to secrecy. After he leaves, Katherine is anxious and I know she thinks about cousin Anne.

I woke in the night. There was a frantic tapping at the window beside my bed and I sat up, thinking for a moment it might be Lettyce. Yellow fingers with long glassy nails were scrabbling to be let in. They smashed through the glass and clutched at my hair. I screamed and woke sweating in bed. I lay wakeful till dawn, my heart thundering in my chest. Dread in my veins.

Surely it must be good that the whole of England thanked God for Katherine on Sunday. That her husband thinks her a pure and loving wife? If only she didn't love Thomas so. If only I could leave. But she does and I can't.

The Time For Dancing

Oh God. I have just spewed up in my mouth. Something dreadful has happened. We don't know what exactly, but we were trying new dance steps in Katherine's rooms when we heard boots pounding along the corridor.

Guards burst in and the head one said, 'The time for dancing is over.' Katherine laughed because she thought it was some sort of joke. She's been expecting a surprise celebration after the church thing on Sunday.

But it wasn't a game. They said she was under arrest and mustn't leave her rooms. She became hysterical and ordered them to tell her why. Then the Merrys decided to become hysterical too.

I tried to calm her, but she clung to me, breathing in little shallow gasps, and I thought she might faint, 'Does he know about Thomas? Who could have told him?' she whispered.

Rumours

Cecily is not locked in with us but, like me, seems able to slip in and out of places without being noticed. She lent me her hood and brown skirt and nobody noticed me. I listened in the corridors and discovered that the King's food-taster, he tests all the dishes for poison, has found out that Katherine had Francis Dereham as a boyfriend before the King.

The King is horrified and in a fury. Maybe, if that is all he knows though, he will be able to forgive her. Or if not, divorce her, or, say the marriage wasn't real, like with Queen Anne. That wouldn't be so terrible.

There is whispering and fear everywhere. So many rumours. Just as I was sneaking back into our rooms, I heard shouting and scuffling from one of the dining halls. Nat Wootton was grabbed, protesting, by two guards and marched away, right past me. How can I tell Merry? No one even knows what he's meant to have done.

Archbishop Cranmer is starting to interrogate people. Some have already been called to the Tower and Cecily and I are sure that is where Nat Wootton is being taken.

I slipped back in to Katherine's rooms and swapped back hoods with Cecily, but I think one of the guards saw us swap. We'll have to be even more careful.

Katherine is saying it is all a big mistake and, if she could only see the King, he will see how silly it all is and be so cross and sorry about her being locked in here.

Cecily came after dinner. Francis Dereham has been arrested and taken to the Tower. He will be put on the rack and tortured for sure. Katherine clung to me.

We just heard that the King is going into prayers in the Chapel Royal. Katherine got up quietly, then ran to the door and fought her way through the guards, like a wild cat. I tried to pull her back but she wrenched free. She ran down the Long Gallery screaming and screaming for Henry to help her…A high, shocking, animal sound. I will never stop hearing it.

The guards caught her and dragged her back, of course, still screaming. We don't know if the King even heard her or if he turned away with a hard heart.

She is still crying and I can't calm her, 'He loved me so much last week, Mattie? How can this be happening to me?'

Will he walk away from her, like he did Anne Boleyn? He loved her passionately too.

Uncle has been summoned back to court. Uncle will sort it all out, thank God. He will help her if no one else can. Surely, at least, he'll make a good divorce settlement and see we are provided for. Maybe I can take Katherine home with me to Norfolk. We have both done everything he wanted us to do.

This afternoon Uncle came. He had scary Archbishop Cranmer with him. We were all sent out and had to listen at the door. Uncle was stern, which made Katherine so agitated she could barely speak to answer his questions. Uncle got up and came to fetch me in.

He escorted weeping Katherine out, which left me on my own with Cranmer. He looks hard at me. The room is dark but for a candelabra placed where he can see me, but I can barely see him…Cranmer smiles, but his eyes are cold like lard, no spark. He asks me how long I have known Katherine. Was I in the long rooms at Lambeth with her?

Did she ever talk to me of Francis Dereham? He pauses. Have I heard what happens in the Tower? Do I know what happens to liars and traitors? Have I heard of the rack? He leans forward and stretches out his white fingers. Painfully wide. I am frozen.

Uncle comes back in. Sees that I am terrified. Fear flickers suddenly in his face too. Uncle smiles at Archbishop Cranmer then waves his hand by his head as if to say, 'she is a simpleton. There is nothing in that head but sugarplums.' So I act blank and dumb as I can see that is what Uncle wants me to do.

A weighted look passes between him and Cranmer, 'She's a feeble-headed child. She knows nothing. Cares for nothing but finery and dancing.' His eyes flash a warning at me. Cranmer gives him a long, slicing look and then lets it go. I am dismissed. My knees are buckling but I curtsey, innocent and simpering.

I waited outside the door as the Merrys were called in, one by one. When Uncle left, I crept out of the shadows, followed him through the anteroom, expecting that he'd tell me what to do next. How he'd help me to get away, to get Katherine away. But he just nodded distantly and passed by, as if to say, 'That is all I will do. I no longer know you.'

Cold fingers clutched my heart. It is a final warning look.
I can see he is frightened. For himself. Not for us. He cares
nothing for us. I am no-one to him now. We were chess
pieces in his game, and now we're on our own.

Archbishop Cranmer came again this morning to see
Katherine. He was acting kind. From what I could hear
through the door, she seemed to be copying out what he
dictated to her. It was all about Francis being her first love
when she was at her grandmother's house.

The door is thick so we could only hear in snatches: 'Treason'
and, 'Betray the King's trust' and, 'Save from the scaffold'. It
was a written confession. But she hadn't written it.

The Merrys are hysterical. Guards just came to take Merry
away. Probably because of Nat. Cecily and I are trying to find
out what is happening. It is so strange to think of Court life
continuing without me and Katherine, where once we were
the centre of everything. I managed to slip out by bribing the
kindest young one with a perfume for his wife. Cecily gave
me her cloak and we slipped into the shadows together.

We heard whispering that Nat is on the rack and one of
the guards was joking about 'The Skeffington's Daughter,
welcoming someone's daughter.' Merry could not possibly
stand that agony. The King always hated Nat. I must be so
careful not to be seen.

The guards stopped as I went in and the young one is in trouble. Someone else in trouble because of me. Now I'll have to get Cecily to slip notes under the door, or in trays of food. Thank goodness for her love of codes.

Thomas Culpepper is out hunting with the King today as usual. Thomas is one of the few people he wants by him constantly. Katherine is desperate for Thomas to remain safe. She really does love him – for the first time in her life she feels something unselfishly. Cranmer seems to know nothing about it yet. We cannot believe it will last.

She lies on her bed clutching the little golden heart brooch.

A coded note from Cecily in the dinner tray to say they are interrogating everyone at Katherine's grandmother's house. All around us terrified courtiers are burning letters and suspecting their friends are spies. Oh Lord, I must keep this journal safe…I have taken the key off my chain and sewn it into the hem of my under-shift. At last a use for all that sewing.

Oh please God may Thomas have had the sense to destroy all her notes and letters.

The King has left Hampton Court. The Merrys and I watched from the window as he slipped away on the royal barge to catch the tide to London. She is lost to him now.

I can't stop thinking about what may be happening to poor Merry Buxton. Is she crouching in a shrinking cage in the dark?

The Worst

The worst has happened. I couldn't get out today, but Cecily whispered through a crack in the anteroom door, 'Francis Dereham was stretched on the rack last night and has told them about Culpepper. Matilda, you must be so careful.' I wasn't sure that Francis knew, but of course he did, and of course he would betray the rival he hated, when threatened with his life. Now all will be up.

I keep thinking I hear stomping boots coming for us. It is a waking nightmare. Will they interrogate me, after all? I must become a shadow: A silly, empty-headed idiot girl.

Thomas Culpepper has been arrested. They came for him as he returned from hunting. They say the King looked away.

Oh good God. I am so frightened. If I were in the Tower… being stretched on the rack. Do they put girls of fourteen on the rack? Or twist them into The Daughter and leave them in the dark? Merry is not that much older than I and they say she is there because Nat was part of a plot against the King, but I know that is foolishness. Would I be able to keep secrets? I never want to have a secret to keep, ever again.

Terror

This morning Katherine couldn't stop crying, nor could we coax her out of bed. Then suddenly she jumped up, wanting to put on her best pink frock, 'I think everything is going to be alright,' she said, 'I just know Henry will forgive me. He can't stop loving me. It's all so stupid...I didn't even know the King when I was with Francis. I mean I was only thirteen...' she gabbled. She has gnawed her fingernails to the quick - and she's so proud of her hands.

Cecily and I keep telling her that if she admits she was promised to marry Francis – Francis even says they had a kind of wedding ceremony – then the King might say their marriage never existed – like with Anne. But she won't listen to us and keeps denying it outright, like Kate caught stealing sugarplums.

As Long As Life Endures

Oh God, they have searched Thomas' rooms and found the letter she sent in April, when he was ill. The one I helped her write. The fool didn't destroy it. Or he loved her too much to. Now all hope is gone. Snatches of it run through my head like a tolling bell.

'...I never longed so much for a thing as I do to see you and speak with you...it makes my heart die to think... I cannot always be in your company...Yours as long as life endures... Katherine'

It is treason. It will break the King's heart. His two favourites: the two people who made him feel young and magnificent. He will be volcanic with rage. But will he imprison her? Exile her to the country? Or kill her? Kill us? 'Yours as long as life endures...'

The stomping boots do come. The guards come to order her to give back all her jewels. Casket after casket of them. They made us strip the rubies out of her ears and the diamonds from her neck. They've arrested lots of the older Ladies, including The Hawk.

Now they tell us she is only allowed to be in two of the eight Queen's rooms. And now, oh God, they are taking all her good clothes. The pearl-encrusted dresses and the jewelled hoods. Even her satin dancing shoes. Then they took Ribbons, too, wrenching him from her arms. He wagged his tail excitedly, thinking he was going for a walk.

Worse still has happened. Cecily says Thomas has been taken to The Tower. He will be put on the rack for sure. Melly whispers that he will be stretched till his arms are wrenched from their sockets. I slap her and tell her to shut up. Katherine is hysterical. I can find no way to calm her.

They've told us to pack. Pinpricks of fear all over. Just a few of us and some servants. We don't know where we're going. I pray God not The Tower.

Before we leave Cecily thrusts a book into my hands: 'Forester's Herbiary'. A book about herbs.

Banished

It is Syon Abbey we have been sent to. To wait. It feels a tormented, sad place.

Katherine won't eat and can't sleep. She is starving herself. Her eyes are huge in shadowy sockets. Our rooms are clean but very bare, with no tapestries and only a small fire. She's been allowed six very plain dresses and six hoods in dark colours.

She's crying so desperately, a guard has just come in to take the sewing scissors in case she might try and slit her wrists. She paces to and fro, all day long, pulling the few simple rings she has left, on and off her fingers, which are red raw. The little golden brooch, which Thomas gave her, is clasped in her hand. It leaves its heart imprint on her palm.

Wearing the drab gowns upsets her. I think she sees how much of her day was spent in dressing and primping for balls and masques. Her own appearance was her creation – her life's purpose. Now she has nothing to distract her. I can't believe I used to care about clothes so much myself.

She is too confused and fearful even to pray. She can't even concentrate when I read to her. She only calms when I stroke her hair and tell stories of her and Thomas, 'Tom is twirling you round and round, in your pink gown, in a rose garden. He's telling you how beautiful you are and feeding you wild strawberries,' I whisper.

She is like a child. It is like calming Kate. I feel so much older than her now, as though she has grown no older since we met. Though she is nearly seventeen now and has lived through so much.

I feel older than when I came to court – but no wiser – I have been as vain and silly and selfish as she has. All for glitter. And fuelled by pride. But who did we have to advise us? Our Uncle? What could she do – a fifteen year old girl with a thirteen year old friend and a madman of fifty for a husband?

I have found underlined words in the book Cecily gave me. The first one is sage. I have to get outside to look for it.

They say they'll let me into the gardens to gather a few herbs for a sleeping draught. I have to be careful lest they think she'll try and poison herself, but they see she has bad headaches from the weeping and fear.

Hope

I found the frosty sage in the herb garden. By it there was a basket of precious valerian and inside, a note from Lettyce:

'Miss Matilda you must get out now. Your mama and sister say so too. Percy can get a small boat to the little pier by the oak. Leave word in this basket under a bunch of lavender so we can see it from the river if the worse comes to the worse and it comes to the Tower…'

Clever Cecily. Clever Lettyce. Percy must have rowed her all this way from the Tower gardens. But how can I leave Katherine now? I can't.

She screams in her dreams when she does sleep – crying out for Thomas and sometimes for me and sometimes for Ribbons.

I too wake in the cracks in the night. Pinpricks of fear and memories of other dreams seep in. A raven in my hair and the ruby throat, are caught up with the padding of Katherine's blistered feet, as she paces our room, backwards and forwards in front of the moonlit window.

I get up, bathe her temples, and lead her back to bed. I tell her Thomas stories. Neither of us admit what we know to be true - that he is being tortured in the Tower and that soon it will be worse for him.

I heard the guards last night saying Thomas and Dereham are both going to be hanged at Tyburn. An old guard was joshing a young one about it, 'They take'em down from the gallows before they're dead, while their legs're kicking and then slit open their insides, so as they can see all their own guts come out and then they cut their heads off.'

I strode to the door and shouted at them to keep quiet and they looked a bit ashamed.

Christmas Day

The saddest day. My family must be so fearful for me.
They say that the time between Christmas day and
Epiphany is when the dead come back to walk…Will we
soon be 'the dead'? To think of last year and Katherine
showered with gifts, dancing and flirting. The prettiest
Queen in Christendom.

They have told us the trial is tomorrow.

This afternoon Katherine was suddenly full of hope. 'I just
know he's going to pardon me and then we'll be let out of
here. That's all I want. He'll be so sorry when he sees me
looking so pale and thin.'

She doesn't want to believe Thomas must have been
executed by now, and she talks as though he were alive
and waiting for her.

'Maybe the King will let us get married after all this is over,'
she said, 'We could have a small house in Norfolk, near you.
And children. I don't even need jewels now. I've got used to
simple clothes. As long as we can have dancing sometimes.
And maybe a few masques with home-made costumes.'

I know Thomas is horribly dead by now. I don't know if she
is going mad but she seems to believe in this simple house
in Norfolk and she even ate something for lunch.

She's not allowed to be at the trial. They are having the trial without her. So it must all be over.

The trial is finished. I heard the guards say that, straight afterwards, the King had asked fifty ladies of the court to dine with him. Did any of those ladies think of his poor young wife pacing the floor of Syon Abbey?

The Tower

I saw them first, coming up from the river. Black-cloaked against the cold. A deputation of lords. Katherine smartened herself and ran to them, full of hope. She didn't understand their formal language. They asked her to sign a confession and an apology and to say she wanted to leave her few dresses to her Ladies.

She was almost light-hearted and thought they meant that when the King sees the apology, he'll pardon her and she'll have all her old dresses back. She fully believes it tonight, and can't stop chattering even as I write this.

'I'll have a simple white silk wedding gown and chains of daisies in my hair...and Thomas shall wear blue and you and little Elizabeth will be my bridal Maids, of course... with cornflowers in your hair...And we'll put flowers round Ribbons' neck...'

But in the early morning they came. I watched the guards stomp up from the river. Her death warrant had been signed. It was to be the Tower. Uncle was there, but his face was grim as death. Even then she fought. She clung to the furniture and screamed out that Henry would pardon her. The guards had to carry her, kicking and weeping, out to the barge. I told them to put her down, 'Walk the last steps with dignity Katherine. You are still their Queen.'

And, like a character in a masque, she did walk the last few steps, leaning on me as she climbed onto the barge. Uncle walked up the gang plank behind us. I looked right into his cold, dead eyes and he turned away from me.

It was a frozen February morning and the river was shrouded in mist. Her crying and pleading was drowned out by the splash of the oars in time to the dismal drum beat. She clung to me and then, as we passed under London Bridge, we saw them. The heads of Thomas Culpepper and Francis Dereham.

Her first love and her last love, on spikes for all of London to see. A seagull pecked at a gelid eye. The colour of candied violets. 'Tom…' She half fainted into my arms.

We entered into the Tower of London by the Water Gate. The way the traitors enter. At last she believed it. Thomas is dead and her life is nearly over. The portcullis swung down behind us. Uncle turned his back on us and was rowed swiftly away from the shadow of the Tower on the dark water, back to Court.

Sir Edmund Walsingham, the Lieutenant of the Tower, greeted us respectfully. We supported her sagging body up the mossy steps. Heard the bleak cry of a raven.

The rooms here are bare but comfortable, though we are both chilled to the marrow. We are inside the Bloody Tower. They asked if there is anything she wanted.

We were all surprised when she asked calmly, 'May I have the block brought in to practise with?'

She wanted to rehearse how to make a graceful, Queenly death. So tonight they dragged the heavy thing in.

We sat close to the fire and she gripped my hand, 'D'you think I'll go to heaven and he'll be there waiting? Or…to the other place? Or somewhere between, where lovers go? Mattie, I keep seeing his eyes staring from the bridge.'

I told her that wasn't Thomas. His soul wasn't there.

'I'm stupid and shallow and vain – I do know that,' she said, '…but I did love him. D'you think that counts for anything?'

I told her all she'd done wrong was to marry a rich, old man she couldn't love, when everyone told her to. I told her to. I begged her to forgive me. I said I knew their souls would be free. We were both crying. I held her and whispered that I knew Thomas would be waiting for her. Though I feel as though I don't know anything at all.

She got up, dried her face, and started to practise how to lay her head on the block. She asked me to blindfold her, as we know that's what will happen tomorrow. She will have to take off her hood and leave her neck bare for the axe. She knelt down, lay her cheek on the wood and stretched out her arms. I couldn't stop crying but she started laughing at the sick, unreal horror of it.

We can hear them hammering outside the window. They are building her scaffold on Tower Green. I slipped out to the garden, saying I wanted valerian so she might get a few hours sleep. I knew from The Herbiary, exactly which bush in the gardens to go to, to find the message. Cecily, Lettyce and Percy have planned it all out, 'When 'tis done, hide behind the first bank of Yew trees. I will be there.'

I lie awake through the night, holding her, writing this while she sleeps fitfully, beside me. Her face on the pillow in the cloud of gold hair, looks so young.

I have just remembered. Tomorrow it is my birthday.

Do Not Forget Me

At dawn we got her ready. They had already come for the block. She was calm as I brushed her hair away from her neck. Just before we left the room, she slipped something into my hand saying, 'Keep it safe for us.'

It was the golden heart brooch. Hide it. Hide it with the key in the hem of my shift. I tucked you, journal into the sleeve of my cloak. White sky, steps, guards, drums. Heart lurching into mouth. I live it again:

She remains calm until we start to walk up the steps to the scaffold on Tower Green and she sees all the people. Court only allowed – but still about two hundred people come to watch her die. Their faces swim before us – so many that we know. So many who fawned and flattered us. Wrapped against the cold in their fine velvets and furs. She swoons and her legs buckle under her. We support her up the steps, 'Pretend it's a masque, Katherine,' I say, 'Walk forward.'

She stands there a moment, looking out at the sea of faces, which begin to blur into the white sky. She thanks the executioner – huge, black-masked – hands him the little purse of money. He cradles the shining axe tenderly. She murmurs something to the crowd.

Something, maybe, about her love of Thomas Culpepper, but her tiny, shaking voice is lost…Her dark gold hair blows in the icy wind.

She grasps my hand, 'Don't forget me, Mattie.'

We tie the blindfold over her eyes and guide her forward, to kneel down and lie her face on the low block. She throws out her arms. Her hair spreads in coils and the axe falls.

I can't look, but I hear the caw of the ravens as the crowd thrill at her head falling onto the blood-soaked straw. I wait just a moment, to see them wrap her poor body in a black blanket, and then I slip away, back into the shadows and through the peacock crowd.

No one notices me as they crane forward to see Kitty Howard's pretty head in the basket.

At the edge of the crowd, eyes frost-blind with tears, I feel my way towards trees. I hear shouts behind me. A harsh cry as a raven flaps up from the grass. I beat it off, its muscled wing catches in my veil and then I begin to run, knowing they've seen me now. Sound of boots on gravel. Don't look round. Boots are gaining on me. Almost blind. Shouts behind me. I weave back into the crowd, flowing now, towards the gates. Heart seizing I find the Yew trees.

I press through the dark, cruel branches and there is Lettyce, her face strained, white. Behind her, Percy.

She thrust a bundle of boy's clothes at me. I slipped you, journal, into the breeches pocket and she helped me pull off my skirts and throw on the rough jacket. I climbed into the wheel-barrow that Percy had ready, and curled up.

Lettyce threw sacking over me and Percy trundled me calmly through the crowd, whistling. Just a gardener's boy, working, on the day of another royal execution. He wheeled me through a maze of pathways, through courtyards and gardens. I felt flagstones and gravel beneath me, give way to softer soil. Percy pulled off the sacking and tipped me out, into the mud. He grinned as I tumbled down the sodden riverbank. He grabbed my hand to pull me up and lead me to a small, waiting boat. Lettyce jumped in after us. No-one spoke. He rowed us, sure and deft, away from the Tower.

We reached a little jetty and Lettyce pulled me ashore. I scrambled up, in my muddy boy's clothes. I struggled, my face red, to find words for Percy, who has risked his job, and probably his life, so many times for me.

There, saddled and waiting, was Caspian. Beloved Caspian. I buried my face in his mane. Next to him was another horse and rider. She lifted her veil. Frances. She had come for me too. Lettyce jumped up behind me on Caspian: 'Stop crying and get riding.' I turned to thank Percy, but he had already cast off. He smiled his warpy smile, lifted his cap and rowed away.

Spring

I am settled quietly at home, grateful to be back helping my mother and Frances and lying reading in my beautiful pear tree. Hunter is a great lolloping dog now and Kate a huge girl. And my new baby brother is called Robin. Cecily is coming to stay with us soon.

Lettyce and I are deep friends, though we never talk of our adventure. My Uncle is perfectly safe of course. He's back at Court again and has cut off all contact with us.

It all feels like a dream now. The masques, the dancing, the secrets, my beautiful, glittering friend…Only this journal remembers the girl who slipped into the shadows. I will keep it for my granddaughters to read some-day. I will pass on the golden heart brooch and they will know its story.

I lie my head back on the bough of the pear tree and drift away, drowsing contentedly.

But suddenly she is here, running through the orchard, running along the passage outside my bedroom, 'Help me, help me…He isn't waiting for me….Help me, help me Matilda.' Those green eyes stream scarlet tears down her white cheeks. Ruby necklet, pale throat, shimmering dress. She's running through the moonlight, amongst the pear trees, on blistered feet. Tapping her bitten fingers at the windows…

And again and again, night after night, Frances shakes me awake as I scream out. For I cannot forget her.

Whenever I close my eyes, she is there.

THE END

Sightings of Katherine's Ghost

As Joanna Denny notes in her book, 'Katherine Howard: A Tudor Conspiracy', many sightings of Katherine's ghost have been reported over the centuries. A figure in a green Tudor dress was seen in what used to be the Rose Garden at King's Manor. She passes through the walls carrying roses, as though on her way to meet Thomas Culpepper.

Hampton Court Palace, where so many of the traumatic events of Katherine's life took place, has a so-called 'Haunted Gallery'. There have been many reports of Katherine's ghost having been seen running, weeping, down the long gallery, to bang on the doors of the Chapel Royal pleading for Henry to help her.

In 2000 two visitors, on two separate guided tours, fainted after feeling something invisible 'punch' them outside the door to the chapel. In December 2003, CCTV cameras recorded on tape a figure in a long Tudor skirt and wide sleeves pushing violently through emergency doors, trying to leave the palace. One of the security guards reported, 'It was incredibly spooky because the face just didn't look human.'

But Katherine hasn't appeared again since. Do you think you might see her if you visit Hampton Court Palace?

Timeline

1509   - Henry VIII is crowned king and marries his
first wife: Catherine of Aragon.

1516   - Catherine of Aragon gives birth to Mary.
Mary later becomes Queen Mary I.

1524/5 - Katherine Howard is born.

1533   - Henry VIII marries Anne Boleyn and divorces
Catherine of Aragon.
- Anne Boleyn is crowned Queen.
- Anne gives birth to Elizabeth.
Elizabeth will later become Queen Elizabeth I.

1535   - Henry falls in love with Jane Seymour.
- Anne Boleyn is beheaded at the Tower of London.
- Henry marries Jane Seymour.

1537   - Jane Seymour dies, after the birth of their son
Edward. Edward later becomes King Edward VI.

1539   - Duke of Norfolk sends his niece Katherine to court.

1540   - Henry marries his fourth wife Anne of
       Cleves. Henry has their marriage declared annulled.
       - Henry marries Katherine Howard.

1541   - Katherine is imprisoned in Syon Abbey.

1542   - Katherine Howard is beheaded at the Tower
       of London.
       - Her body is buried in a grave in the chapel next
       to Anne Boleyn's.

1542   - Henry marries his sixth wife Catherine Parr
       who outlives him.

1547   - Henry VIII dies.
       - Henry's son by his third wife Jane is crowned
       Edward VI aged nine.

1553   - Edward dies.

1555   - Duke of Norfolk dies in his own bed of
       natural causes.
       - Henry's daughter by his first wife Catherine is
       crowned Queen Mary I.

1558   - Queen Mary dies.
       - Henry's daughter by his second wife, Anne Boleyn,
       Elizabeth, is crowned queen. She rules for 45
       years. Elizabeth never marries.

Glossary

Page 1: Necklet - A necklace.

Page 3: Winding sheet - A shroud or sheet that bodies were wrapped in for burial.

Page 5: Pomander - A small, ornate spherical metal container with holes in it, often hung from a chain at the waist. They were filled with sweet-smelling herbs, believed to ward off the plague or, "the sweat". Matilda uses hers to sweeten the air around her at court. They could be very pretty and finely made, if worn by wealthy courtiers.

Page 5: Coverlet - A bed cover.

Page 5: Kirtle - An underskirt. See Pages 36-39 where Matilda describes all the sections of her new court dress.

Page 5: Syllabub - A dessert made from cream beaten with sugar and wine.

Page 6: Mixing medicines - In the sixteenth century the daughters of a noble household, amongst many other domestic duties, would have learnt how to prepare medicines. They would have looked after the younger children when they were ill. They would have learnt to recognize and grow herbs in the family 'kitchen gardens' which would have a 'physic border', for medicinal herbs.

Valerian, for example, was often used to help sleeping and feverfew for headaches and the brain of a hare, when ground up and applied to the gums, was believed to help babies with teething pain.

Pork or hog fat was often used as a base for ointments with herbs and tinctures mixed into it.

A young girl like Matilda, who was able to make and apply popular remedies of the time, would have saved the family a lot of money on expensive doctors or 'physicians'. Many ingredients might seem disgusting but many herbs, such as lemon balm and lavender are still used today. It must have been one way for clever girls like Matilda to use their brains and creativity.

Page 7: Marchpane - Early name for marzipan. It was made with almonds, sugar and rose-water and coloured with vegetable dyes such as saffron for yellow and parsley for green. It was modelled into elaborate shapes such as flowers and animals and castles.

Page 9: Doublet - A man's close-fitting jacket.

Page 11: Tallow - A fatty yellow substance made from sheep or cattle fat, used for making cheaper candles than proper wax ones.

Page 13: Chatelaine (means Mistress of the Castle in French) - A fine chain worn round the waist, with keys, a pomander and useful tools like scissors and thimbles etc. hung from it.

Page 26: A galliard and other dances - A galliard was a slow, stately dance and a volta a fast, lively, up-tempo dance. A pavane was a slow, processional dance.

Page 52: Christendom - Encompassing all Christians throughout the world.

Page 59: Sanded - When letters were written with quill feathers dipped in ink, sand was shaken over the finished letter to blot up the ink so it would not smudge.

Page 85: Bear-Baiting - Rich and poor people in Tudor times enjoyed cruel spectator sports such as this. A bear, often with its teeth removed, was tied to a post, where it would be attacked by dogs trying to tear its throat out, while it defended itself with its paws.

Page 140: Skeffington's Daughter - Also known as The Scavenger's Daughter. One of the many gruesome torture devices in use at the Tower. It was named after Henry VIII's Lieutenant of the Tower, Sir Henry Skevington. It was a metal band wrapped round the prisoner, who was made to crouch with his knees by his shoulders, whilst the band was tightened gradually with a massive screw.

Page 168: Water Gate / Traitors Gate - Matilda refers to her entry into the Tower of London via the Water Gate and its portcullis (seen in picture scrapbook 4). It later became famously known as Traitors Gate and is known by this name today, where you can see it at the Tower of London.

Picture Credits

Anne of Cleves / Hans Holbein the Younger / Collection:
Superstock / Photographer: Peter Willi / Getty Images

Portrait of Thomas Howard, 1539 (oil on wood)/ Hans
Holbein the Younger / Collection: The Bridgeman Art
Library / Getty Images

Portrait of Henry VIII (1491-1547) aged 49, 1540 oil
on panel / Hans Holbein the Younger / Collection; The
Bridgeman Art Library / Getty Images

Portrait of Marie de' Medici as a child / Agnolo Bronzino /
The Bridgeman Art Library / Getty Images

Horse Galloping / Photography by Deborah Raven /
Photonica Collection / Getty Images

Anne Boleyn, 1534 (oil on panel), English School,
(16th century) / Hever Castle, Kent, UK / The Bridgeman
Art Library

Black and white illustrations + annotations on montages. Laura Barrett

Louise Robinson

Louise Robinson

Photographer: Bertie Miller
Assistant: Ben Etridge
Retouching: Cosmetic Ink

Acknowledgements

Many books were very useful to me in researching Matilda's Secret. Joanna Denny's biography, 'Katherine Howard: A Tudor Conspiracy', particularly, was one I returned to again and again.

The exact date of Katherine Howard's birth is unknown. Joanna Denny's view is that Katherine was 15 when she first met Henry in 1539, putting the year of her birth at 1524 or 1525. Denny points out that chroniclers of the time refer to Katherine as being exceptionally young. It seems very likely, in her view, that she was a girl of 15 rather than a woman of 20, which had been a view more traditionally held by other Tudor scholars.

Thanks to Frances Cain - big boss lady and mastermind behind the A GIRL FOR ALL TIME® world, and to her daughter Samantha Cain. Thanks also to Rebecca Wolff who edited the book.

Photo-montage pages. Thanks to photographer Bertie Miller and to our models Sadie, Thea, Maya and Brittany.

A special thank you to Louise Robinson for her inspiring and magical cover artwork.

Biography

Sandra Goldbacher is a screenwriter and director. She is twice BAFTA nominated for her feature films – 'The Governess" starring Minnie driver, "Me Without You" starring Michelle Williams and "Ballet Shoes", a BBC Christmas adaptation of the children's classic by Noel Streatfeild, starring Emma Watson. Sandra is endlessly drawn to stories about the complicated interactions of young women. Sandra lives in London with her husband and son.